In Silence Sealed

A Novel
by
Eleanor LaBerge

PublishAmerica
Baltimore

First printing

All characters in this book are fictitious, and any resemblance to real persons, living or dead, is coincidental.

PublishAmerica has allowed this work to remain exactly as the author intended, verbatim, without editorial input.

ISBN: 978-1-61582-691-9
PUBLISHED BY PUBLISHAMERICA, LLLP
www.publishamerica.com
Baltimore

Printed in the United States of America

The human heart has hidden treasures,
In secret kept, in silence sealed.

Charlotte Bronte:
"Evening Solace"

Dedication

I wish to dedicate this book to gay men and women educators who have been compelled to live their lives "in silence sealed." In particular, I wish to honor those who have been among our schools' most inspirational teachers.

Remembering my school days, I was taught by two women whose devotion to their profession inspired my own career as a teacher at both the senior high school and university level. Later, as my colleagues and my friends, they confided their deep commitment as a lesbian couple. If they had been compelled to acknowledge their orientation, their careers would have been in jeopardy and four generations of students would have been deprived of their extraordinary talent.

This is a work of fiction. The characters are fictional. However, I must admit that in the shadows of my imagination, I was influenced by the memory of two extraordinary women who are no longer with us. *In Silence Sealed* is meant to honor them. M M McD and M E H, I hope you have found each other in eternity.

E.LaB

Acknowledgments

I appreciate the proofreading and suggestions of my husband, Earl, and that of Jean Jacobson, Celine Nichols and Joan Nykriem—"straight" friends who compassionately defend the rights of the gay and lesbian community. I also want to thank Colonel Grethe Cammermeyer for graciously consenting to read *In Silence Sealed,* I was heartened by her comment that the book may resonate with some who have experienced choices similar to my characters. Special thanks to my daughter, Chavaleh, for technical help in electronic transfers of the manuscript.

Part One

Sacramento, California: 1941

"Can you believe this road?" Alice Barnes complained to her assistant as she swerved to avoid another deep pot hole.

"From the looks of the house they probably can't afford the upkeep," Thomas Miller said.

The house was in need of paint, and the weed choked front yard showed gross lack of care. As they approached the front entrance, the door opened and a stout woman as unkempt in appearance as her surroundings met them on the porch.

"The kid's inside. Come on in."

"Are you Thelma Erickson?" Alice asked.

The woman nodded. "I'm the one who called you, and I can tell you I'm sure as hell glad you came out so soon."

"We try to respond to reports immediately," Alice said.

Thelma led them through a cluttered living room to the kitchen where there was an accumulation of unwashed dishes. "She's in here."

The toddler sat in a high chair frowning at a bowl of canned peaches. She had a piece of bread and jelly in one hand, most of which was on her face and fingers. A bit more was in the dark curls that framed her face. She was a pretty child with blue eyes and lashes thick and dark as her hair. "I don't like them peaches!" she said pushing the bowl which clattered to the linoleum floor.

Thelma was swift to grab the child, yanking her roughly from the chair. Alice reached for the infant fearing that the woman was about to shake her. Ignoring the fact that the child's face and hands were sticky and her bib had remnants of what was left of a soft boiled egg, Alice took her. Startled, the little girl stopped fussing. Thelma bent to pick up the spilled fruit. "Hey—watch your step, the brat made a slippery mess." Taking a dish towel she merely covered the syrup. "It'll wait. You must have a way with kids, lady. You saw how she squirmed and howled when I picked her up. She won't even let me comb her hair without screaming."

"We've had some experience with these cases," Alice said, thinking that the woman hadn't made an effort to comb the snarls from the child's hair for some time. Turning her over to Thomas who had brought a blanket, she asked "Do you have the letter and certificate you spoke of on the phone, Mrs. Erickson?"

"Sure do. What I got in the mail yesterday is right here."

Examining the envelope's contents, Alice said. "A birth certificate is very little for us to go on." She turned to Thomas. "Her name is Winifred. I see the mother's name is Rosalie Jones, and the father is a George Eldridge."

"Rosalie's' right. 'Jones' is fishy, don't you think?" Mrs. Erickson remarked.

"Perhaps. When did she leave Winifred with you?"

"She asked me if I could take care of her for the weekend so she could move to a place closer to work. That was two weeks ago. I didn't hear no more 'til I got this letter. No return address, just a Los Angeles postmark."

"Had you known her long?"

"I didn't know her at all. My kid Barbara knew her from before. Barb's a waitress at Andy's diner over on the highway. This Rosalie dame stops in there with the kid and tells her she needs a sitter for a few days. That's how I got her."

"Can you think of anything else? Perhaps something that might help us locate the father?"

"One thing. Barb said that when she was here a couple of years ago she told her that she was going to get married. She said her boyfriend was up at a school in Washington. He had something to do with forests or some such."

"Do you know which school?"

"No, but it was in a town with a funny name—'pull' something."

"Possibly Pullman. Washington State University has studies in Forestry," Thomas offered as he walked Winifred back and forth to keep her from fussing.

Alice smiled at him appreciatively. The young man had a gentle manner with children. "That might be helpful," she said. She handed Thelma her card. "In case either you or your daughter hears from Rosalie, please call me."

The child made little objection to being taken by strangers. She seemed interested in looking outside the car window from her vantage point on Thomas' lap. "Cows!" she squealed as they drove past a field.

"What about over there?" Thomas asked as they passed another pasture.

"Horsies!" she cried pointing.

"She seems to be a smart little cookie," Alice remarked to which Winifred turned to look at her. "Cookie! Can I have a cookie?"

"And verbal," Thomas laughed, reaching in a case for a Vanilla Wafer. "I've learned to come prepared!"

A call to Washington State University confirmed that a George Martin Eldridge from Bellingham, Washington had been a student at the school He had received a Bachelor's degree and then a Masters in Forestry. Alice was unable to obtain a current address, but the registrar gave her the family home address and also put her in touch with his fraternity. Its alumni chairman was able to supply more information as well as the fact that George Eldridge was now married to a Marion Philips. He also told her that George's father was deceased; his mother's name was Agnes, and that he had a sister, Helen.

The phone rang as Helen Eldridge was on her way out the door to meet Harriet and Vernita, friends with whom she planned a vacation trip to British Columbia. Agnes was in the garden and Helen could imagine her elderly mother rushing in to answer if she didn't take the time to pick up the receiver. That was inviting a fall and possible injury.

When her conversation with Alice Barnes concluded, Helen sat on the chair by the hall telephone and tried to sort out all she had heard. The child couldn't be left at the Sacramento children's facility if she were indeed George's daughter. "Damn that George," she muttered to herself. Shortly after he had completed his undergraduate degree, their father suffered a fatal stroke. George came home to Bellingham for the funeral and then left abruptly. Helen had been furious with him. At the time she couldn't understand why he had to return east of the mountains when he had several weeks before summer quarter when he would start his graduate work. For his mother's sake he should have delayed until the fall, but he had insisted he needed to return to school. Was it to marry this girl if he knew she was in a family way? Or had there been a wedding? George's name on a birth certificate was no proof of marriage. Helen hoped that if there had been a secret marriage to this Rosalie there had been a divorce. Unpleasant as that fact might be, it was better than facing the problem of bigamy!

The immediate problem was the difficulty of communicating with her brother who was employed by the National Park Service in the wilds of Montana's Glacier Park. In emergencies the Park Service could contact those in the wilderness camp areas, but it was by two way radio, a park service operator relaying both sides of the conversation. There was no way Helen wanted this private family matter to be heard by strangers. First she needed to tell her mother.

After calling her friends to postpone their meeting due to a "family emergency," Helen steeled herself for the conversation with her mother. She found her in the garden digging. "Mother," she scolded. "We have a hired man to do the heavy work! I thought you were in the greenhouse potting seedling tomatoes."

12

"Since when do you check up on me? I never do more than I should. Inactivity is inviting infirmity. But you didn't need to worry, dear. I was about to go in and get ready to keep an appointment to have my hair done."

"Mother, prepare yourself for a shock."

It took two days for George to reach a telephone after the Park ranger radioed him that there was a family emergency. Helen answered the phone.

"Hey, Helen—what's wrong? Is mother ill?"

"No, she's fine, but…"

George interrupted angrily. "I hope you've got a damn good reason to call me down from the mountain."

"Yes, George, I have a very good reason."

When she repeated all the information given her by the official from the children's society, there was silence on the line. "George, do you know this Rosalie?"

"Yeah, I knew her."

"Obviously in the Biblical sense," Helen said drily.

"How old is this child?" George asked hoping that the dates would let him off the hook.

"She is two years old."

"Oh, God," he sighed. "That would be about right. We only dated a few times in my senior year, but one night we got carried away and…"

Helen interrupted him. "I don't want to know the details, George."

"Well, she took the whole thing seriously as if it were some sort of proposal. When I left right after father's funeral it was so I could let her know the relationship wouldn't work, and marriage wasn't going to happen."

"She probably knew she was pregnant," Helen said.

"If she did she didn't tell me. When we broke up she went to California. She should have told me."

"She quit school?"

"No. She wasn't a student. She worked at a café in town."

"George, the woman I spoke to made every effort to find her, but she had no more information than a brief note and a birth certificate which gave the mother's place of birth as Los Angeles. Do you have any address?"

"I think I might be able to find her through her sister in Pullman. She was living with her. I'll call while I'm down here and let you know."

"Marion will be upset by this news—understandably," Helen said. "It will be a shock to discover you two have a ready made family."

"She'll forgive me. But Helen, we can't take the kid. The way we live there's no way we can take care of a two year old!"

"Mother and I have already discussed this. We plan to drive to Sacramento and bring her home."

"I'm sorry this has complicated things for you and mother. "We won't be able to leave Glacier until the park closes and hey, be careful crossing the passes. After Medford it's a bad road and there can be ice even at the beginning of June."

"We'll manage, George. Call us as soon as you have more information. Here's your mother. She's eager to speak to you."

Agnes had accepted the news of a granddaughter calmly. "I think, dear, now that we have talked to George we should leave for Sacramento immediately and bring the little girl home."

"It's a long drive, Mother. I'm sure Mildred will drive with me."

"Nonsense. I'm perfectly able to go with you. I'm sorry that you'll have to disrupt your plans to go to Canada with Harriet and Vernita."

"The girls will understand."

Agnes suppressed a smile. It amused her when Helen referred to Harriet Lamberton and Vernita Brown as 'the girls.' Harriet, a history teacher at the college where Helen was chairman of the Education Department, was in her forties as was Vernita who taught high school English. The two women had shared a home for a dozen years.

Agnes' Bridge Club ladies whispered that there was a relationship to which ladies of refinement would not give a name. Agnes, unwilling to gossip, encouraged her group of card players to concede that it was practical for two unmarried teachers to share expenses. After all, both were stalwart members of Saint Andrew's Episcopal Church. Still, talk like this worried Agnes on behalf of her daughter. Helen was frequently the third wheel or part of a foursome with her friend Mildred when that friend's physician husband was otherwise occupied.

"I don't think it would be right for me to go to Canada and leave you with the responsibility of a toddler," Helen said. "And to tell you the truth, when Mildred told me she couldn't go because Lloyd planned to take his staff for a cruise through the San Juans, I wasn't eager to go, but I didn't have an excuse to back out."

When Agnes and Helen told her the news, Annie O'Hara, the live-in Eldridge family helper, made plans to bring the crib and other stored furniture from the attic to a spare room for the baby. Annie had been with the Eldridge family since Helen and George were children. She had come to them when she was a fifty year old widow to be a live-in mother's helper. She kept the house, helped in the kitchen and provided companionship for Agnes. When Helen went off to school in the east, George, ten years younger, was in grade school. When William Effinger died, Annie remained with Agnes even though Helen had given up her apartment and returned to the family home.

"Annie, it's not as if this is a permanent arrangement," Helen protested. "I'm sure the child won't be with us for long once George and Marion come for her."

"Well, we can be prepared, and they could be needin' these things eventually. Jimmy next door promised to get another boy to help carry everything that's heavy. We'll be ready for the wee lass when you bring her here."

Helen left her mother to pack for their journey while she took the Buick to the garage for a safety check. The mechanics checked the tires, changed the oil, and assured her that the car was in excellent condition. That job done, she headed south on Chuckanut Drive, the picturesque route by the bay which led to the northern Skagit Valley. She needed to confide in the one person whose discretion she trusted absolutely, her friend Mildred.

Mildred Sutherland lived on the waterfront drive several miles from the Bellingham city limits. Lovely as the setting was, Helen could not imagine that living there would be worth enduring Mildred's façade of a marriage. Dr. Sutherland would be in his office at this hour, thank heaven. Helen would not want the man to be privy to any of the Eldridge family's personal business. She knew Mildred would not betray any confidence, and in the situation Helen now faced, it was a comfort to know she would have her sympathetic support.

Mildred prepared tea and the two friends sat outside on the deck that overlooked the cove on the waters of the northern Puget Sound. "Helen, dear, what a shock!" Mildred said after hearing the news. "Look on the positive side. You may find it a blessing to have this little girl until George and Marion come for her."

"I'm unlikely to see it that way, but Agnes is thrilled," Helen said without enthusiasm. She avoided talk of children with Mildred whose two girls had always taken precedence in their friendship. They were grown now and living 3,000 miles away—one in Hawaii and one in Boston. Helen made a point to seem fascinated with the two grandchildren that Andrea, Mildred's older daughter, had produced. The other girl, Patricia, worked for a travel agency in Hawaii. It irritated Helen to hear Mildred gush that Pat should find herself a "nice young man." How her friend could wish the state of matrimony seemingly just for its own sake when Mildred's marriage was nothing short of a disaster, Helen couldn't fathom.

Even before the time his girls had left home and were on their own, Dr. Lloyd Sutherland made no effort to conceal a relationship with his receptionist which had gone on for years. Mildred had turned to Helen for the understanding she had never experienced with Lloyd. To Helen's continuing frustration, Mildred would not consider a divorce. Appearances were important to her, and she continued to play the part of the perfect hostess and helpmate.

After a second cup of tea, Helen said she had to get home. "Agnes is eager to pack. She'd leave this afternoon if she had her way. But I have to wash my hair. We'll get an early start tomorrow."

The task of washing her hair was not simple. It had been twenty years since Helen had permitted it to be cut. She parted it in the middle, and braided two long strands, winding them around her head helmet fashion. Both her father and brother had thick dark hair. Helen's was thin and fine, an unremarkable light brown with a hint of red which saved it from being mouse colored. For years Mildred had tried to convince her friend that a cut would be easier to maintain. Privately Mildred believed that a less severe style would soften Helen's sharp features.

Helen telephoned Alice Barnes to assure her that she and Agnes would leave for California the next day. "We had to take our car to the garage for a thorough check. It's a long drive," Helen explained.

"We're happy that Winifred will be cared for. The child has been a delight at the home. She's a precocious little thing!"

The trip took two long days with a stop in Medford, Oregon.

After Helen and Agnes had taken Winifred from the Children's Protective Agency, they made a stop to give Thelma Erickson a check of compensation for her care of the child. Helen approached the house while Agnes remained in the car holding Winifred.

Thelma answered the door. Even though she had expected the visit, she had made no effort to be presentable or straighten the living room. The place was redolent with a pungent smell Helen didn't recognize until she saw several cats. Thelma wore a faded house dress, no stockings, and slippers. She was as slovenly as Helen

Eldridge was neat. Looking at Helen, Thelma thought, *typical skinny old school maid.*

"You have any kids?" She asked Helen.

"No, I do not," Helen answered, tempted to tell the woman it was none of her business.

"Well, thanks for this," she said pocketing the check Helen gave her. "The kid's a willful brat. Good luck with her." Thelma said.

Helen was relieved to get back to the car. "Mother, you would not believe the condition of that woman's house. And the smell! She keeps cats, and never cleans. Frightful," she shuddered and drove from the property as quickly as dodging the holes in the road would permit.

"Did you give her enough?" Agnes asked as they drove away.

"More than enough. She told me that we were very generous. She even smiled."

Agnes remarked that money seemed to have the power to transform many an unpleasant attitude. Helen agreed. It was rare for her mother to make a remark even remotely unkind, but in this situation it was justified.

The first thing Agnes did when they checked in to a downtown Sacramento hotel was to give Winifred a bath, feed her and settle her for the night. The child had taken an instant liking to her grandmother who held her and sang her to sleep. Helen left her mother to this task while she went to a department store to purchase new clothes and blankets. She found the infant toy department and bought several things for the child's amusement on the drive home.

"Winifred seems to be a docile child," Agnes said.

"Not according to that awful woman." Helen remarked.

They looked at the child, asleep on a hide-a-way bed the hotel had supplied. She clutched a fuzzy teddy bear Helen had bought. Her dark hair showed signs of natural curls that framed her chubby cheeks. Her slightly upturned nose had a faint sprinkle of freckles.

"She's the image of George as an infant," Agnes said as she gently removed the child's thumb from her mouth and covered her with a soft blanket. Agnes had bottles of milk and juice prepared and Helen had bought a few jars of Gerber's and a box of Pabulum which they could heat on the portable hot plate Helen had packed for the trip.

It took two days to reach Seattle, and although Agnes and Helen were exhausted, they drove three more hours north to Bellingham. Amazingly, Winifred was a good traveler, napping much of the time on the road. At home Annie was ready with a play pen, toys from a trunk in the attic, and a nourishing supper. Winifred didn't seem upset by her new surroundings, and was happy to settle in her crib for the night.

"You'd think the wee one would have a hard time adjusting to strangers," Annie commented.

"She didn't seem to object to our taking her from the children's home," Agnes said. "I think she must be accustomed to changes in her surroundings."

"Aye, she's likely to have been taken from pillar to post," Annie commented.

Agnes smiled at the expression. She had always wondered about the derivation of "pillar to post." Perhaps it was an Irish saying.

"Well, thank heaven we're safely home," Helen said as the three ladies closed the door of the room Annie had arranged for the baby. With the coming of Winifred, Annie was, as she put it, "Gettin' me second wind! The wee lass put new life in these old bones!"

"This is a significant change in our lives," Helen remarked. Agnes gave her a searching look. There was no sign of displeasure in her daughter's expression or her voice. Agnes had been concerned knowing that her daughter preferred an orderly life with little variation and no surprises. Agnes was determined not to require Helen to make major changes in her normal routine.

When Agnes took Winifred to the children's section of a downtown department store, the toddler made her preferences clear. She shook her head at a yellow quilt and pointed to another pink and lavender one. She chose stuffed animals over baby dolls, and was remarkably fascinated by picture books. "I'd say that Winifred is much more precocious than willful," Agnes remarked to Helen when she returned from shopping.

Each evening before bedtime Helen or Agnes would read little Golden Books and in a short time Winifred would choose her favorites. She would also finish the last lines of poetry from Mother Goose rhymes.

"It's almost as if she can read," Agnes said.

"I don't think she's that bright," Helen laughed, "but she seems to be an exceptionally intelligent little girl!"

Winifred had been in Bellingham for seven months before George called to say that the higher elevations of the park had now closed for the winter; he and Marion would be coming to Bellingham.

"What have you learned about Winifred's mother?" Helen asked, "And are things all right between you and Marion?"

"Marion has been wonderfully understanding. And no, I haven't heard anything from Rosalie's family, but her sister in Pullman gave me her other sister's Sacramento address. I wrote to her months ago. So far there's been no reply."

"When do you start for home?"

"We're leaving early tomorrow from Kalispell, and it shouldn't take us more than three days."

Before leaving Montana, Marion and George had decided that they would have to tell Agnes and Helen that they could not take Winifred. For George and Marion to take the child, George would have had to find work other than the park service. "I don't know what else I could do, and the reason I majored in forestry was to avoid a desk job." Marion admitted that she was not prepared to care for a toddler under the primitive circumstances in which they lived most of the year, and most of the responsibility would be hers. Agnes was sympathetic. It wasn't fair to spring the idea of a ready made family on the girl. After serious consideration, the family decided that Winifred should remain with her grandmother and aunt permanently. Marion tried to be conciliatory. "When Winifred is old enough she could spend vacation time with us if the park department assignment is suitable."

Agnes was uneasy about future legal problems. Rosalie might at some time in the future make a claim for her child notwithstanding the fact she had abandoned her. The concern ended with tragic news from Rosalie's sister, Linda. George had given the Bellingham telephone number in his letter to her, and she called while George was still there. She told him that Rosalie had died more than a year ago after swallowing an overdose of aspirin.

"She came to me here in Los Angeles when she found out she was pregnant," Linda told him. "When she began to date the man she planned to marry, Rosalie and Winifred were still with me. When her fiancé discovered that Winifred was hers and was illegitimate, he wouldn't marry her, and he was appalled that she had concealed the fact from him. Then my husband wasn't happy that Sis and her baby had stayed here so long. He told Rosalie she had to get her own place. We had an awful scene. Rosalie was almost hysterical. She took Winifred and left."

"Poor kid. Why didn't she tell me she was in trouble?"

"She wouldn't even tell us who the father was."

"So where did she go?"

"Sacramento. She called me from what she said was a dump of a motel out on the highway and told me not to worry. She had a temporary job waitressing in a diner. I asked her what she was going to do about Winifred when she was at work, but she said she had found a baby sitter—I had no idea who it was. When the police called to tell us that Rosalie had died, they said there was no sign of a baby. Until your letter I had no idea who you were or what had happened."

"Could Rosalie have taken too many pills by accident?" George asked.

"I don't think so. She was terribly upset and depressed, so I doubt it was an accident."

"Winifred's too young to ask questions, but in the future… Will your folks want to have her? She is their granddaughter."

"When I told my father that Rosalie had died he didn't even ask about the baby. He doesn't want any reminders of Rosalie. He's a hard and unforgiving person. When she came home and admitted she was pregnant he threw her out of the house which was why she came to me. Mother is not well. She would have taken Rosalie's baby, but she didn't dare suggest it to my father."

George reported the conversation to his family. "It's a sad story, but we can be grateful that Winifred is safe and loved."

"We should see our lawyer about legal custody," Agnes said.

Agnes looked out of the window at her shrubs and lawn which were covered with frost. "We're in for a cold winter this year," she said to Annie who was dressing Winifred in her warm coat and leggings before they drove to Sunday services. The telephone rang and Helen answered. It was Mildred.

"The radio! Turn on your radio!"

Helen went to the upright Philco in the living room. The ladies listened in shock to the news that Pearl Harbor had been attacked by the Japanese. Annie started to remove Winifred's coat, but Agnes said, "I think we should all go to church and pray for our country."

The following spring when Winnie was three years old, George and Marion took advantage of the Easter holiday to drive to the coast. Marion endeared herself to Agnes by helping to hide Easter eggs in the back yard without a word of complaint about a succession of rainy days.

"I'm used to inconveniences!" Marion told her mother in law. "George and I spent most of last year in a park service cabin that had no electricity. We had a wood stove for heat and cooking, a little stream for water when it wasn't frozen, and when it was, we melted snow. We had gas lamps for light, and no indoor plumbing!"

George had been refused when he volunteered for military service because of a heart murmur, and it seemed he was to be permanently stationed at Glacier Park. George was playful crawling about with Winifred on his back as she cried "More horsie! More horsie!" Observing the loving attitude of George and Marion toward the child, Agnes wondered if they might reconsider giving up custody. It would be George's right, of course, but she dreaded the separation. Marion brought up the subject. "Winifred is such a delightful child. I truly wish our work permitted us to have her, but realistically it doesn't."

"If you had a child of your own, surely you would have managed," Agnes said.

Marion hesitated, and finally she replied. "I can't have children. George and I discussed this at length before we married. I didn't believe it would be fair to deprive him of a family, but he convinced me it didn't make a difference to him. Of course that was before we knew about Winifred."

The subject was dropped. Winifred remained with her grandmother and aunt. Agnes worried that the child had no association with children of her own age. Her circle of friends were grandmothers, but either their grandchildren lived out of town, or were much older than Winifred. Helen's friends were unmarried with the exception of Mildred, and her children were grown. Both Agnes and Helen tried to make up for the lack of playmates. Winifred didn't seem to miss what she had never known. Agnes was both surprised and delighted that Helen was devoted to her niece, and enjoyed spending time with her. By the time Winifred was five she knew her letters and was reading from the Little Golden Books her aunt and grandmother bought for her. Winifred's development pleased Helen who had registered Winifred for the fall term of the college kindergarten program.

Grandmother taught Winifred perfect table manners. She learned not to gobble her food, to use utensils properly and never, never to speak with her mouth full. When Helen and Agnes took her to restaurants, the child's manners were always praised.

"Such a quaint little thing," a waitress once said.

When she entered kindergarten, for the first time in her life Winifred was in the company of children her own age. She had no idea how to play with them. The children soon realized that Winifred was "different."

"You talk funny!" one boy sneered.

"Yeah! And you're a fatso!" Another added.

"Where did you get all those freckles?"

The pecking order left Winifred at the very bottom, the brunt of teasing. By the time she was in the third grade her nicknames were "Plumpkin," "Fatty," and "Nose in the Air." Winnie had no idea how to fight back, so she withdrew into stoic silence. The fact that her teacher praised her achievements and deportment added still another insult: "Teacher's Pet." After school, in the refuge of her home, Winifred's tight shell of reserve opened and a happy child emerged. Neither Agnes nor Helen was aware of the little girl's miserable school days.

Helen was an accomplished equestrian and kept a horse at a local riding academy. Winifred learned to ride, and participated in the horse shows held at the stables. Several afternoons each week, Winifred and Helen would go to the academy. Mildred had boarded her daughters' horses there, and she had kept one of their geldings so she could ride with Helen. She was happy to have Winifred ride him. He was well schooled; an ideal mount for a beginner.

When Winifred was ten years old, Victoria Anderson came into her life. One Saturday after having spent the morning riding with Helen, Winifred was bouncing a ball on the sidewalk in front of her house. A huge moving van arrived in the driveway next door. The house had known a succession of renters, but had been vacant for several months. The original owners, the Kashiwagi family, had been forced to abandon it when they were taken to Puyallup, Washington where they were restricted to the internment camp for Japanese. Grandmother called Winifred in telling her that she might be in the way of men carrying large pieces of furniture. "You may watch from your room," Agnes told her.

The moving van was parked for most of the day. When it had gone, a car replaced it in the driveway. The Eldridge family had just eaten dinner and Winifred was helping Annie dry the dishes. Helen was not at home and Agnes was in the back yard garden when the doorbell rang. "I'll answer it!" Winifred said.

On the front porch she met a tall woman dressed in a sweater and slacks. Beside her was the most beautiful little girl Winifred had ever seen. She had golden blond curls, and when she smiled there were deep dimples in her rosy cheeks.

"Hello!" the lady said. "I'm Mrs. Andersen, your new neighbor. Is your mother at home?"

"My grandmother is—I'll call her."

Agnes came to the door wiping her hands. "Please come in! Forgive me, I was planting some marigolds."

"And I've been unpacking all morning. I don't usually come calling in slacks! I'm Lydia Anderson, and this is my daughter, Victoria. She'll be in the fifth grade at the college school. My husband has accepted a position in the science department at the college."

"How nice," Agnes said, "My daughter Helen is the chairman of the education department."

Agnes urged Winifred forward. "This is my granddaughter, Winifred. She'll be starting fifth grade at the college school too."

Winifred smiled shyly. "Would you like to see my room?" she asked.

"I'd love to!"

Victoria was enchanted by Winifred's collection of horses. "Oh, I dream of having a horse," she said.

"My aunt has a horse. We ride all the time. I'll bet she'd let you come with us."

Not only were the horse figurines interesting to Victoria. She was impressed by Winifred's collection of books. That was the beginning.

As the summer went on, the girls were constant companions. Helen took them riding, the girls played games indoors when it rained, roller skated on the sidewalk when it was sunny, and played Chinese checkers endlessly. During the hot days of summer they would sit at a card table in Winifred's shady back yard sipping lemonade and playing with paper dolls or coloring books. Winnie had never been interested in dolls, but when she saw that Victoria was, she suggested that they put card board boxes together like a stage and use dolls as puppets.

With the physical activity of skating and general play, Winifred trimmed down. When her aunt took her to buy school clothes, for the first time she bought regular sizes instead of those on the "chubby" rack. The trip to the department store for shoes and school clothes was a reminder that summer vacation was going to end in just a week. Winifred dreaded the first day of class.

The boys eyed the pretty new girl and didn't even think about teasing her. The most popular girls decided to recruit her for their special group. Watching the boys' reactions and the fawning girls, Winifred's heart sank. Lunch hour on the first day of school, the class filed downstairs to the cafeteria where hot lunches were prepared in the adjoining kitchen. Long tables and stools filled the room. Winifred's grandmother had packed a lunch for her in a brand new lunch box. Victoria stood in line for a hot plate lunch. When she carried hers from the line, the 5th grade girls called to Victoria and moved their stools to make room for her. Winifred watched from where she sat alone at a table near the door.

"Thank you," Victoria said without hesitation, "but I'm sitting over there with my best friend."

Winifred was stunned, and grateful. "Thank you," she whispered when Victoria settled beside her. If the girls wanted Victoria to join them, they soon realized that they had to include Winifred.

The girls' close friendship continued through grade school, but ended suddenly during the summer before high school. The two had spent the first three weeks of their vacation with George and Marion in Yosemite Park. At the end of this happy time, Victoria returned to discover her mother packing up things from the kitchen and dining room. "Your father has accepted a full professorship at the University of San Francisco," she told Victoria. "You'll be able to see some of your old friends in California."

Winifred had never felt more miserable than she did on the day the Anderson's car drove away. She and Victoria pledged to write and Mrs. Anderson promised to invite Winifred to visit. "We'll plan a trip to Disney Studios," she said hoping to cheer the girls.

In an effort to shake Winifred out of her misery, Helen bought a gentle mare so Winifred could ride her own horse rather than Mildred's. Winifred, Helen and Mildred frequently rode on an old railroad trail above Chuckanut Drive. Before Victoria became her friend, Winifred had hoped for a horse of her own. The joy of having a real friend dampened her enthusiasm for a horse. But trying not to hurt her aunt's feelings, she managed to pretend great delight in the gift. As a substitute for Victoria, the horse fell short, but Winifred would never let her aunt know that.

Helen's friend, Vernita Brown was Winfred's freshman English teacher. After several essay assignments which were written in class, Miss Brown made a point of speaking to Helen. "Do you have any idea how gifted your niece is?"

"She's an excellent student. Obviously we've known that."

"But her writing is far beyond her age. Have you begun to plan for college?"

"Indeed. Agnes and I are hoping she'll be accepted at Wellesley, my alma mater."

"I don't see that there would be any reason why she couldn't qualify."

When Winifred entered her sophomore year at Bellingham High School, she added an elective, the school newspaper. The teacher advisor recognized her talent and recruited her for the debate team which she also sponsored. Winifred was no longer teased by her contemporaries. She was respected as an honors student, and the debate team was strengthened by her skill. By the end of the spring semester she was appointed the coming year's senior editor of the school paper, *The Bellingham Bugle.*

The paper and the debate team gave Winifred a new sense of belonging. Aunt Helen was no longer the center of her social activities. There were times when Winifred didn't go riding with her aunt because she chose instead to be with her friends. Agnes noted the frequency of Helen's "silent treatment" when her granddaughter had plans other than those Helen had arranged.

"I don't know why we keep a horse for Winifred when she clearly has other interests!" Helen complained. When there was a play at the college, Helen wanted Winifred to attend with her and Agnes. But Winifred said she had plans with a few of her friends from the school paper to see a revival of "Lost Horizons" at the local movie house. Helen's reaction was to snap at her. "Well, forget about us. Go and enjoy yourself." Agnes tried to mediate. "She's growing up, Helen. She needs to be independent, and it doesn't mean that she loves us less. You used to worry that she didn't know children her own age."

Winifred's group of editors, reporters and debaters were dubbed "The Brains" by students. They shrugged off any implied slur and flaunted their differences. They called themselves "Young Citizens for Freedom of Thought." They followed politics and world affairs, and despised their contemporaries whose school life revolved around sports and sock hop socials.

During the summer of 1955, the newspaper staff and debaters met to plan the next year and voice their opinions about current events. Nelson's Drug and Soda Fountain was the favorite haunt for these conversations partly because of its location near the college where older students gathered. It was also the place where they could smoke. When Teresa Hamilton, the only other girl in the group, first offered Winifred a cigarette, she confessed that she had never smoked. "My aunt would have a conniption fit," she said.

"Well, don't tell her!" Teresa offered a Chesterfield from her purse.

Winifred puffed hesitantly, and her friends told her she looked like a ten year old kid sneaking her first puff behind the family garage. "You draw in the smoke like this," Jerry Oldfield said, inhaling and then letting the smoke come out through his nose.

Winifred tried, but choked and sputtered. She coughed so hard she thought she was going to embarrass herself by throwing up.

"Take it slow," Teresa encouraged.

By the end of the summer Winifred became adept at faking the inhaling process. She would suck in smoke and let it come out through her nose as the others did. Soon she perfected the art of blowing a smoke ring to her friends' approval. Grandmother noticed the smell of tobacco one day and Winifred said, "The news staff and debaters meet at Nelson's and the place is always full of smoke from the college students."

The excuse placated Grandmother, but from that time on Winifred would leave her jacket outside on her bicycle's handles so it wouldn't smell of cigarettes. She also had plenty of Life Saver mints on hand. She didn't dare carry her own cigarettes, but would persuade one of the college students to buy a pack which she entrusted to Teresa. Winifred knew that Aunt Helen would have a fit if she caught her with a pack, and Grandmother, though more tolerant, would certainly not approve.

The week before their junior year began, Winifred's school group was gathered at their favorite booth with milk shakes and smokes. Winifred had just blown one of her famous smoke rings when she looked up and saw Helen inside the door staring straight at her. Helen watched Winifred crush out the remains of her cigarette, but turned on her heels and left the store without saying a word.

"Jeez, Winifred, you're going the get it when you get home," Jim Logan said.

Teresa said, "If looks could kill we'd all be dead—and you would have died twice!"

Helen had left Nelson's without purchasing the item she had come for. She was angry and embarrassed. How many people—Ben Nelson certainly—had seen Winifred smoking? The hurt she had felt for months when Winifred chose to spend more time with her friends flared. She had accepted that it was natural for a teen age girl to want to associate with her peers, but to discover that Winifred had not used good judgment regarding the friends she chose was disturbing. Why had she not seen this kind of rebellion coming? And what else was Winifred doing behind her back?

Instead of driving directly home, she took the road to Chuckanut drive. Mildred was in her garden gathering a bouquet of the last summer roses. Always happy to see Helen, she hurried to the car. "I thought you'd be in your office all day! Come in, I just baked some brownies; we can have tea." She hesitated when she saw that Helen was upset. "Helen dear, what's wrong?"

"A great deal. I do need some tea to settle my nerves."

Mildred listened to Helen's description of Winifred with her friends. "Helen, don't let this become more than it is—normal adolescent experimentation."

"Did your girls ever do anything so distressing in public?" Helen challenged.

"If they did, I didn't know about it, mercifully."

"Are you suggesting that I ignore this incident?"

"No. You must surely talk to Winifred and explain why you are upset with her."

"I think not. She is out of control and I need to nip this rebellion in the bud."

"I don't understand, dear. How are you going to correct her behavior if you don't talk to her?"

"There has to be a decisive response, and I think I know exactly what needs to be done."

By the time Helen returned home to report Winifred's public defiance of all the values she had spent years instilling in her niece, she was committed to a course of action. Agnes was distressed with what she felt was a precipitous decision, but was unable to alter her daughter's plan.

Winifred knew that she had committed a serious transgression. Miserably she prepared herself for the worst as she rode her bicycle home after completing outlines for the first edition of the school paper with her friends. She was certain that Helen would forbid her to meet with her friends outside of school, and might even report the incident to their teachers. When she arrived at the house, she saw Helen's car in the driveway, but Helen was in her room.

Winifred couldn't let what happened be concealed from Grandmother. If Aunt Helen hadn't told her, she felt she must. Agnes' response was to put her arms around Winifred and hold her close. "Honey, while I think you are too young to start smoking, and I don't think it was wise for you to do so in public considering you aunt's position in the community, this will not come between you and me. I love you, and don't forget it."

"I won't smoke again—I promise!"

Helen came downstairs with a small suitcase. She didn't refer to what she had seen at Nelson's, but she was not smiling when she spoke to Winifred.

"Grandmother and Annie need help canning the fruit Harriet and Vernita brought us from Yakima. I would appreciate it if I could count on your being home this weekend rather than running off with your friends. I have to drive to Portland."

Winifred said she'd be happy to help, but was puzzled when Grandmother said goodbye to Helen with tears in her eyes. What, Winifred wondered, was there to be sad about Helen's going somewhere for the weekend?

Helen returned from her trip late Sunday afternoon. Monday was Labor Day and she left the house for the academy to ride with Mildred. She did not invite Winifred to come along. Winifred noticed that Aunt Helen and her grandmother barely spoke. Tuesday morning when the high school staff attended what they called Teachers' Institute, Winifred was up and dressed early preparing to meet with the paper staff to review the mock-up for the first edition of *The Bellingham Bugle*. Aunt Helen stopped her on her way out the door.

"I want you home no later than noon," she said.

"Sure! We're just going to be at school." Winifred hoped this would assure her aunt that she wouldn't be at Nelson's smoking.

"Very well." Helen told Agnes that she would be home sometime during the morning to take care of what we need to do."

With this cryptic remark she left. Winifred was puzzled that Helen had not confronted her directly with the punishment her transgression seemed to demand. That she was displeased was obvious. So what did Aunt Helen expect her to do by way of reparation? How about stitching a big red letter "C" for Chesterfields on her sweater like Hester Prynne's scarlet letter "A" for adultery? It would be amusing to do that and maybe the joke would coax a smile from Aunt Helen. Smoking wasn't adultery and it sure wasn't murder. But Helen probably felt that what Winifred had done was a form of murdering her reputation with her friends and faculty members who were customers at Nelson's.

After Winifred left the house, Agnes climbed the stairs to her granddaughter's room. Helen had given her a list of clothing to pack, things already in the girl's wardrobe which would be appropriate for St. Ann's Academy in Portland, Oregon where Helen had enrolled Winifred. Agnes had begged, cajoled, and given every argument she could to dissuade Helen from the drastic measures she was determined to take. Helen had refused to listen to Agnes' opposition and demanded her mother's loyalty. Agnes didn't continue to pursue an argument she knew she could not win. Agnes was left with an ache in her heart and the knowledge that she would miss her dear Winifred terribly. Annie helped her pack the suitcases, and both had shed tears.

While she was in Portland, Helen had located a store that supplied uniforms for private schools. She found everything that would be required except for a special order of a blue monogrammed jacket. Headmistress Elizabeth Hopper said there was no immediate need for the dress jacket as long as Winifred had the school sweater. Everything Helen ordered would be delivered to the school and be in Winifred's room when she arrived. The uniform was simple and practical. A brown and blue plaid pleated skirt, tailored white blouse, brown and white saddle shoes to be worn with blue cotton socks, a blue sweater for everyday use and the jacket for more formal occasions. The girls would wear white gloves when visiting outside of campus, and a blue hat which completed the outfit.

Agnes and Annie packed two suitcases including gym clothes and shoes. They folded new towels and Agnes put in a special bar of perfumed soap and talcum powder. She wrapped framed pictures of herself, George and Marion, and one of Winifred taken the year before with Helen and their horses. Agnes doubted that the one of Helen would merit an honored place in her niece's room. From her apron pocket Agnes drew out a sealed envelope with Winifred's name on it. She slipped it in the second suitcase, and then with a heavy heart snapped it shut. In the note she had tried to explain how sorry she was and to confide that she did not support Helen's extreme punishment. Her letter would make it clear to Winifred that she was on her side.

Winifred was home by noon as she had promised. When she turned the corner and approached the house, she saw a van with a sign painted on the door, "Saint Ann's Academy," Portland, Oregon. It was parked in their driveway. Her curiosity turned to horror when she saw two of her suitcases next to its rear door. Inside she saw her grandmother with tears in her eyes and two women. Both wore tailored navy blue suits with an emblem "St. Ann's Academy" emblazoned on their jackets. Winifred couldn't speak. She stared at her aunt and then looked into her grandmother's tear filled eyes. "What's happening?" she asked, the words sticking in her throat.

"It's the result of what has happened," Aunt Helen said stiffly.

One of the women, confused by the obvious tension, said brightly, "You will find the Academy a very challenging and rewarding experience, Winifred."

"The hell I will!" Winifred cried, the first time she had uttered a swear word in the house. "I'm a senior editor of our school paper, the president of the debating team, and I'm already rewarded by the fact that I have earned a 4.0 average in a very challenging school!"

"Your transfer has been arranged," Aunt Helen said. "You have been enrolled at St. Ann's Academy."

"We will need to be leaving," the younger of the women said, wondering how it was that the teenager could be surprised by the transfer. She was anxious to depart this puzzling family confrontation.

Winifred, in shock, was ushered to the academy's van. This couldn't be happening! "Grandmother..." she began, looking beseechingly at Agnes.

"In no time it will be Thanksgiving vacation and then Christmas— you'll be home..." Her voice quavered. She began to reach out to embrace Winifred, but the girl had turned to face her aunt. "I will hate you for this as long as I live!" she said with cold fury, and stormed out of the door. Winifred's turning away from her and the hurt in her granddaughter's eyes was like a physical blow to Agnes. Helen didn't wait for the van to leave the driveway before retreating to her room and closing the door. Agnes watched from the window in the living room for a last glimpse of the child she had loved and nurtured for a dozen years. She had tried her best to defend Winifred. "All teenagers rebel..."

Helen would not accept any defense and would give no credence to Agnes' arguments. "What I see in this situation," Helen said, "which you'd like to call a minor rebellion, is that Winifred has disgraced the family, and more than that, she seems to be easily influenced by the group she calls her friends. If this is an indication of future behavior, it needs to be nipped in the bud."

"Helen," Agnes pleaded, "she hasn't disgraced the family. She made a mistake. The extreme punishment you are proposing…"

"I'm not proposing, Mother. She will be transferred to St. Ann's Academy and that's the end of it."

Years before, Agnes and Helen had agreed that Helen should make decisions involving Winifred's education. Now Agnes regretted that she had so little to say in this important step. Helen's retribution for what she thought was a black mark against her reputation, was cruel. It was not proportionate to what Agnes saw as a childish prank. Had her daughter even considered what this high handed action would mean to her mother? Helen felt free to go off with her set of friends and leave Agnes alone, but Agnes had always had Winifred's company. Now she would be alone, the companionship of a weekly bridge club, garden society meetings, and an ailing maid was not enough to sooth a broken heart. At least she had written the note to Winifred to let her know that there was absolutely nothing the girl could do to take away from the unconditional love she felt for her.

The drive to Portland took eight hours with a brief stop for dinner. The faculty members took turns driving. The two women, Miss Tate and Miss Harris, attempted to make conversation with Winifred, but the girl was too hurt and angry to make small talk.

Miss Harris, who was driving, looked at her companion with a slight roll of the eyes. All they knew was that Elizabeth Hopper, headmistress of St. Ann's, had requested that a new student be picked up in time for the new semester.

Miss Tate was an experienced higher mathematics instructor who was liked and respected by her students. On the way north she and the young second year English teacher, Miss Harris, had remarked to each other that it was indeed unusual for Miss Hopper to ask two teachers to make a mad dash to pick up a pupil whose guardians should have made arrangements for transportation.

"St. Ann's Academy is highly rated," Miss Harris said to Winifred hoping that the girl would talk to them so they could help defuse her anger.

"Our coming was a surprise to you?" Miss Tate asked as she turned in her seat to look at their passenger.

"I had no idea," Winifred said. "I'm sure your school is an excellent one, but Bellingham High School is also well known for academics. I believe we could match any of your achievement test scores." Winifred spoke with courtesy, but firmly. It wouldn't be fair to blame these teachers for what had clearly been her aunt's arrangement.

"Really, Winifred, you'll learn to love St. Ann's and you'll find companions who are equal to your academic level."

Winifred paused before responding. "But how would either of you feel if suddenly your headmistress decided to ship you off to teach in San Francisco or Seattle where you knew no one and without your consent? Of course you're adults, and no one would disrespect you by doing such a thing. But how would you feel, really?" She challenged.

"Damned rotten," Miss Harris exclaimed, and all three laughed.

During the remainder of the drive Winifred told the pair how she had been caught smoking and how she had planned to apologize and do anything she could to make up for it. "I would have sworn on a ten foot stack of Bibles never to light a cigarette again. I didn't get a chance; Aunt Helen beat a path to Portland and arranged the whole thing. So here I am."

"We're so sorry," Miss Tate, said.

Miss Harris interjected, "I hope we can keep this exchange of confidences between us three? It's a policy of the Academy that the staff should keep a reasonable distance between us and the students."

"Absolutely I will not betray your kindness. I didn't expect such understanding and I'm really grateful."

"We have a school paper, *The Clarion*," Miss Tate said, "a senior girl is managing editor, and one of my colleagues in our English department, Miss Walker, is advisor. She'll be your junior journalism teacher, and I'll bet after she knows your background she'll recruit you for the paper." She thought to herself that she would speak to her colleague as soon as the opportunity presented itself.

The conversation and exchange of confidence didn't cool Winifred's anger, but it helped her put the situation in perspective.

"Don't slack on your class work to get back at your Aunt Helen," Miss Tate counseled.

Winifred listened, startled by the woman's comment. She had thought of using failing grades as the ultimate protest for Helen's high handedness, and this insightful remark seemed almost as if this teacher had read her mind.

"You must be a mind reader," Winifred said.

"No," Miss Tate responded, "but I'm not so ancient that I don't remember what it means to be a bright teenager with no power over unfair decisions made by adults."

"You've heard the expression 'cutting off your nose to spite your face,' " Miss Harris added. "Don't do it. It might make your aunt angry, but it would hurt you more."

Winifred settled into studies at St. Ann's Academy. It was fortunate, she thought, that the boarders were already paired in the dormitory, Winifred was assigned to a room by herself only slightly larger than her grandmother's pantry, but it suited her. She needed to be alone to work through the devastating changes in her life.

Miss Tate approached *The Clarion's* advisor, Miss Walker, with a word to the wise about the new student. It hadn't been necessary. Miss Walker was impressed by Winifred's first letter to the editor and suggested that she participate in the school newspaper as an extracurricular activity.

By the time Thanksgiving vacation came, Winifred had found her niche at school with the staff of the paper as well as her classes. She would have preferred to stay at school during the holiday, but couldn't bring herself to be so selfish when she remembered the letter Grandmother had put in her suitcase. She had replied at once telling Grandmother that she was sorry she had behaved heartlessly the day she had left for Portland. Each week she wrote home, but she never included her aunt's name on the envelope. George and Marion were going to be in Bellingham for the holiday, and Winifred thought that there would be safety in numbers. She was to take the train to Seattle's King Street Station where George and Marion would meet her.

She would not let Helen think that she had accepted the transfer, but secretly she had fallen in love with the academy and its students. Barbara Grove, the senior editor of *The Clarion*, had inspired Winifred's confidence. When she heard Winifred's story of seeing the van and being whisked away to Portland, she was curious. What had this girl done? She wondered if she had been caught necking with some boy.

"What on earth did you do?" She finally asked.

Winifred told her. Barbara smiled enigmatically. "Well, goodness gracious," she said with mock primness, "I can certainly understand. After all, smoking is much worse than anything else, isn't it? —Like necking in the back seat or murder, perhaps?"

The girls laughed, but it wasn't the end of the subject.

The Saturday following the exchanged confidences, Headmistress Elizabeth Hopper left for a meeting of private school administrators in San Francisco. After the school van had passed through the gates of the academy grounds, Barbara knocked on Winifred's door. "The staff of *The Clarion* invites you to your initiation," she said.

"Initiation?"

"Yes. We are very selective about whom we include in our inner circle. Come with me, but first you must be blindfolded."

Winifred went along with the ritual, and let herself be led up one hall and down another, up one flight of stairs and then down two. Thoroughly confused, she came to a halt in front of a door where the sound of a furnace could be heard within. The door opened and once she and Barbara were inside, the blindfold came off. Winnie saw five girls, surrounded by clouds of smoke from the cigarettes they were smoking.

"Here," Virginia, one of the reporters, said. "Have a Lucky Strike!"

On the train on her way north to Seattle Winifred smiled as she replayed the scene in her mind. She felt affection for her new friends and it was nice to be so enthusiastically accepted. Not only were there infrequent clandestine visits to the boiler room in the basement of the academy, there was the "Listerine Celebration." When report cards came out at the end of the first quarter, *The Clarion* girls met in Angela's room. She had little paper cups on her desk into which she divided the contents of a small Listerine bottle.

"Gee, girls, does the initiation continue with the elimination of bad breath?" Winifred asked.

"Absolutely. Cheers, girls!" Angela raised her cup and swallowed. Expecting the sting and unpleasant taste of mouthwash as a possible continuation of her initiation, Winifred took a gulp, and then choked and sputtered.

"It's 80 proof brandy!" Barbara laughed.

There was barely half a jigger for each measured out, but enough to cause Winifred's nose to tingle.

The empty Listerine bottle was entrusted to different girls before trips home. There was such a small amount put in it, no parent would be suspicious or notice the liquor was missing. It was done in a spirit of mischief.

When the second round was offered months later, Winifred raised her paper cup and said, "Here's to you, Aunt Helen!"

Winifred spent most of her time with her grandmother during the vacation. She, together with George and Marion, drove downtown to see the traditional Christmas decorations which were in place the day after Thanksgiving. Helen didn't join them. The preceding day at dinner there was lively conversation, and Winifred answered questions about St. Ann's, but would not show enthusiasm in front of Helen. She had confided to Grandmother that she really loved the school. When Helen would ask a pointed question about curriculum or teachers, Winifred would smile and direct her answer to others. During the three days of the holiday Winifred managed to say not one word to Helen directly. To her satisfaction, she saw that it annoyed her aunt. However, before she left for the academy, Grandmother took Winifred aside and gently told her that she understood her feelings, but please, don't bring the same anger home for the Christmas holiday.

Winifred hugged her grandmother and promised she would try to make peace between Helen and herself. "Or at least a truce," she said.

"That's all I can ask for," Grandmother said.

After Winifred had left with George and Marion who planned to drive her to Portland, Helen didn't conceal her displeasure with her niece's behavior. Grandmother said "I don't blame our Winnie for being slow to forgive you."

"Winnie! Hadn't we agreed years ago that we were not going to use nicknames? At one time you wanted to call her 'Freddie!' And 'Winnie' sounds like what a horse does, spelled differently, of course."

In a rare moment of sarcasm Agnes said icily, "I wouldn't want your horse to take umbrage."

On the way south from Bellingham, George and Marion were curious to know why Winifred had decided to switch schools. "We thought you liked Bellingham High School, Winifred," Marion said.

"I didn't decide. Aunt Helen did." She told them what had happened and why.

"Well, Winifred," George said, "I have no right to put in my two cents worth, but for the record I think that Helen's reaction stinks. For what it's worth, I'm on your side, but I think it would be best if I didn't interfere— unless you want me to pressure Helen to let you come back?"

"Gosh, no. I love St. Ann's." She then confided the story of the boiler room, but decided that the Listerine bottle would remain secret.

George asked, "What about next summer? We're certain to be at Glacier Park and as you know there's plenty of room at the house we bought on Flathead Lake."

"Remember the wonderful taste of fresh caught Dolly Varden trout?" Marion added.

"I sure do, and I'd love to spend the summer with you. But…"

Marion didn't need Winifred to finish her sentence. "You would be reluctant to leave your grandmother alone."

"Yes. Did you notice that she seems much older? And she's lost weight."

"Weight she didn't have to lose," George agreed. "Mother didn't look well. It was probably the stress of wondering when the fireworks between you and Helen would begin!"

"Grandmother told me that Aunt Helen's going to a class reunion at Wellesley as soon as the college year ends. She said she planned to stay afterwards to visit some friends she knew in school."

George said, "So she's going to spend a whole month away from Mildred?"

Winifred looked puzzled and Marion shot a warning look at her husband as she said "What your father means is that Helen usually includes Mildred on trips."

"Well, I hope Aunt Helen hasn't said anything mean to her!"

"I'm sure not," Marion replied. "Dr. Sutherland is hosting a group of doctors from back east along with their wives. Mildred needs to be hostess."

Later when Winifred had been delivered to the academy, Marion scolded George. "I know what you were implying, but you forget that Mildred is Helen's normal friend. After all, she has a husband and two children."

"Come on, Marion. You know that Harriet and Vernita are the most infamous lesbian couple in Bellingham! And the four ladies are

41

thick as thieves. Besides that, Helen would walk through fire for Mildred."

"That doesn't make her a lesbian."

"Granted it's not a certainty, but I'd give you odds of 100 to one that I'm right."

"She's your sister, George. You could at least give her the benefit of the doubt."

"I've never thought of Helen as my sister. Ten years between kids is a long time. She went off to college when I was seven. She was just a relative that came home once in a while."

"In other words she was a stranger to you."

"That didn't prevent her from trying to control my life. She thought Forestry was a useless major and told me it was my obligation to prepare myself to take over our father's business."

"Didn't you have a minor in Business Administration?"

"Yeah, I gave it up. All it did was bring my grade point down. I was grateful that the Eldridge Natural Gas Meter Company put us through college, but I couldn't see myself behind a desk. At dad's funeral Helen tried to convince me to take over, but I wouldn't even discuss it with her. Actually, selling the company and retaining shares set us all up for life."

The next insult Winifred aimed at her aunt was when the half year report card arrived. Winifred was at the top of her class; had been given honors in every subject; her deportment was excellent; and Miss Hopper wrote a personal note which said that she believed Winifred to be a rare asset to St. Ann's Academy.

Helen opened the envelope and read the report, but red splotches appeared on her face, and she slammed the card on the dining room table. "This is unforgivable!" She said as she left the room.

Agnes looked at the card and smiled. Just above Miss Hopper's comment, Winifred had drawn a cigarette with smoke coming out of it. Grandmother didn't know that Winifred had been tempted to write, "Put these grades in your pipe and smoke it."

The school year went more quickly than Winifred had anticipated. She made an effort to spend Christmas in an atmosphere of civility anxious that she give her grandmother no more worries. They exchanged many confidences during her time at home.

"When we drove to Portland that first time, it didn't take much time for me to know that it wasn't going to be such a horrible place. I told Miss Tate and Miss Harris what had happened, and I said something to the effect that Helen was the wicked witch of the west. Then I heard Miss Tate whisper, 'witch spelled with a B.' She didn't realize I had such keen ears, and Miss Harris gave her a look that would kill, but from that moment I knew I had friends." Grandmother had smiled at the story.

After the ten days of the holiday break, Grandmother had put her arms around Winifred and said, "You were wonderful, dear. I love you."

These were the last words she would hear from her beloved grandmother. Winifred looked forward to her summer homecoming. Helen would have left for the east coast, and Winifred was determined to do all she could to make the summer visit enjoyable. Grandmother wrote to tell her that she had made reservations at a downtown Seattle hotel for a little vacation trip. Winifred had her yearly report card in her purse. It fairly glowed in the dark with praise from the staff and Headmistress Elizabeth Hopper.

Agnes had promised that she and one of her friends would meet the train from Portland. When Winifred arrived at Seattle's King Street station, she searched the crowd for a familiar face. The train was on time, but it was a long drive from Bellingham, so she claimed her luggage and sat in the lobby waiting patiently. When two hours had passed, she called home. There was no answer. If anyone would know what the delay meant, it would be Mildred Sutherland, but there was no answer at her home. Distressed, Winifred didn't know what she should do. It was now four hours from the time she had arrived in Seattle. Then she saw Mildred fairly running into the station. She put her arms around Winifred and said, "Oh, my dear, I'm so sorry…"

At the hospital where her grandmother had been taken after suffering a stroke, Winifred stood outside the intensive care room looking at her grandmother. With all the IV lines and the respirator, she couldn't have recognized her. A nurse permitted Winifred to enter the room and take Grandmother's hand. She bent over and whispered, "I love you. I'm here," but there was not the slightest reaction. Reluctantly, she returned to the waiting room to pray for a miracle.

There was no improvement during the night, and in the early hours, Grandmother died. Mildred, who had waited with Winifred, couldn't persuade her to stay at her home while they waited to contact Helen. Winifred expressed her gratitude, but persuaded Mildred that she would rather wait at her own house. Sitting by herself in the living room, her anger with Helen surfaced. She had been responsible for the stress that had affected her grandmother's health. Winifred's resentment had smoldered for over a year, but now it blazed. She did not want to see Helen; neither did she want stay in the family home. It was a dead and empty place. Annie was no longer with them. She recognized that she was no longer a help to Agnes, but a burden. Annie now lived with her daughter, and when Winifred had visited her during Easter holidays, she seemed to have failed remarkably in just a few months.

Winifred sat in the dark living room trying to absorb all the implications of her grandmother's death. One thing she knew. She did not want to remain here. She wrote a note to Mildred telling her that she had taken a bus back to Portland until the funeral. She knew Mildred had already contacted George and Marion, and had put in a call to Wellesley that Helen was to telephone her as soon as she had checked in for the reunion. There was nothing to keep her from leaving. Mildred hadn't liked the idea of Winifred's being by herself; she would certainly object to her traveling to Portland alone. But after all, Winifred was almost seventeen and perfectly capable of taking care of herself. Above all, she did not want to have to face Helen, and she needed to be alone with her grief.

There were things in the house that she might need—birth certificate, for one thing. She was to take a driver's training class in the coming year and it required proof of legal age. Rather than spend the summer with Helen, Winifred decided she would ask to stay in Portland for summer classes.

She went into Grandmother's room to search her roll top oak desk. She found a file with her name. There was a sealed letter in Grandmother's hand with her name on it. She also found her personal journal which had not been packed with her things when she was shipped off to St. Ann's Academy. Grandmother had sealed it with Scotch tape which Winifred took to mean that it had not been read. How typical of Grandmother to respect her privacy. If Helen had seen it, she suspected that every word would have been scanned. She set both the journal and the envelope aside. In a bank envelope there was $500.00 cash along with the savings account book that she and Grandmother had held jointly. The cash had a note attached which said "For Winifred for any emergency." She wondered if Grandmother had a premonition that something was going to happen to her.

When she went upstairs to the bedroom which had been hers for so many years, Winifred saw that there was a new quilt in the pink and lavender shades she loved. There were new curtains, and a matching scatter rug. Clearly this had meant to be a surprise. This gesture of love brought more tears.

On the dining room table downstairs Winifred found an unopened letter from Wellesley addressed to her. Inside there was a congratulatory letter of advance acceptance for the fall of 1962, a year and some months away. She would be sent more information before the time of freshman orientation. This was Helen's doing. She had not consulted her niece; just gone ahead and applied for her. Transcripts would have been sent, but the academy secretary received so many requests for these on behalf of upper level students, they would have been forwarded without question. As far as the office staff at the academy was concerned, it would have been assumed that she had applied.

Winifred put the letter in her purse. She'd consider her academic future later. She wasn't sure that she wanted to accept. Certainly she would not have wanted to be so far from her grandmother had she lived. The college in Bellingham had a good reputation for undergraduate work, and the local school would be a logical choice notwithstanding the fact that she didn't want to have Aunt Helen looking over her shoulder like a watchful Doberman.

The city bus stopped just a block from the house, and it went downtown past the Greyhound depot. Winifred purchased a ticket to Portland. With the money her grandmother had left her in her pocket she would be able to take a taxi from downtown Portland to the academy. On the way she wondered if she should just use the money and go far, far away. Let her family and friends wonder what had happened. Who would care, really? Her emotions told her to run, but her common sense told her that this was not the reaction of a young adult, but of a silly adolescent. Then she remembered the note from Grandmother and opened it.

My dearest girl,

Try to remember all the good and happy years we have shared, and also keep my love in your heart.
It will always be there for you, deep in your soul, never to leave you. I love you.

Grandmother

It was late evening by the time a taxi brought Winifred to the academy's front entrance. The building would not be vacant since many of the boarders' families worked for the government overseas. The school would be open for summer studies, and it was unlikely that the rooms would be filled. The dorm matron welcomed her, surprised that she was back so soon.

"Something came up." Winifred offered no more information, and went directly to the room she had left only early that day. Barely fifteen minutes had passed before there was a knock at the door. Headmistress Hopper stood outside.

"Come downstairs with me, Winifred. The heat is off up here and we'll be comfortable in my study."

Elizabeth Hopper knew that there was tension at Winifred's home because of Helen Effinger. There must have been something traumatic to bring the girl back to Portland so quickly. The Headmistress ushered Winifred into her sitting room and asked if she had eaten.

"No, but thank you, I'm not hungry."

Miss Hopper sat forward in her chair and met Winifred's eyes. "All right. Now tell me what has happened."

After Winifred had told her, she said, "I'm so sorry. I know you were close to your grandmother. Obviously, you are still angry with your aunt, but isn't it a bit heartless to leave her alone at this time of mutual grief?"

"She isn't home. She's back east at her Wellesley reunion. Our friend Mildred left a message for her to call Bellingham. Mildred also contacted my father."

"Do you know when the funeral will be?"

"Not yet. Aunt Helen and my father will be the ones who will take care of that."

"But you are going to attend?" Winifred didn't answer. "You don't want to be there for your aunt's sake?"

"She was part of the stress that killed my grandmother."

47

"You may be right, and you may be wrong. I would like you to be a more compassionate person than to let your anger control your judgment. Will your grandmother's friends be at her memorial?"

"Oh, I'm sure they will be. She has many friends—the garden society, bridge club, and there were acquaintances from all sorts of committees she served on."

"All of these friends knew you, and were aware that your grandmother virtually raised you?" Winifred nodded. "Then don't you think that they would believe you dishonor her memory by being absent?"

The simple logic of her headmistress' analysis of the situation defused Winifred's anger. "I wasn't thinking clearly." Tears began to fill her eyes.

"I am confident that you would have changed your mind once you were over the initial shock of your grandmother's death. I would like to attend the funeral with you, together with one or two of our faculty. Is that agreeable to you?"

"Miss Tate and Miss Harris?"

It was settled. Miss Hopper said, "I never understood why your aunt requested a special late admission to St. Ann's. Would you share the reason with me?"

Winifred told her, admitting that she had been caught smoking.

"Let me understand. You had no idea that you were to transfer to St. Ann's Academy before Miss Tate and Miss Harris came for you?"

"I had no clue. I saw my luggage beside the school van, and that was when I knew something was up."

"And this is what made you angry with your grandmother and your aunt?"

"I was never angry with Grandmother! But I was furious with my aunt. And she hasn't stopped trying to control me!" Winifred took the letter from Wellesley from her sweater pocket.

"This is remarkable, Winifred. Early acceptances are rare, especially before your senior year. This is a great honor."

"But I didn't apply! In spite of the fact that I dreaded being home with Aunt Helen, I had decided to go to college in Bellingham so I could be close to Grandmother. This letter is just another manipulation typical of my aunt."

"I believe I understand. Perhaps I should not say it, but I am in sympathy with you. Your Aunt Helen showed very little respect for you, and a lack of faith in you. She doesn't work with girls your age as I do. It doesn't seem that she understands a young person's need to be her own person, which would be a reason for rebellion which is, in most cases, a sign of growing up. Of course I don't condone your smoking behind your guardian's back, but then if I reacted in the same way, I'm afraid the boiler room girls would have been expelled long ago!"

"You know about that?" Winifred was shocked.

"Of course I know. It is my job to be aware of what is going on with my girls. Your group doesn't break the rules very often, and thank God you don't parade around Lloyd Center in your school uniforms amid a cloud of smoke! If there had been such blatant disregard for the school's reputation, I would have reacted much differently."

Winifred was amazed at Miss Hopper's forgiving attitude. She was also thankful that the Listerine bottle was still a secret. She made herself a promise that this dangerous tradition had to be stopped.

The next day Miss Hopper asked to see Winifred again. She suggested that she write a letter to her aunt expressing her feelings and, if not making an apology which wouldn't have been sincere, at least she could leave an opening for reconciliation in the future.

Part Two

Winifred returned to the academy after the funeral. She had been prepared to change her mind about summer school if Aunt Helen had offered the olive branch and asked her to remain in Bellingham. Instead, Helen spoke to Miss Hopper and agreed that it would be best for her niece to attend St. Ann's summer session. In spite of the feud which had separated her from her aunt, Winifred was hurt. George and Marion offered to have her for the summer, but she had already decided to enter an advanced placement program at Portland College for which Miss Hopper had given her a recommendation.

In July, Andrew Fleming, the Effinger family solicitor, asked to meet with Winifred. Since she was involved in summer school, he asked his son who managed the Seattle branch of the firm to travel to Portland. Arthur Fleming Jr. brought the news that her grandmother's will had been read and she had left a generous legacy to Winifred. Most of the bequest was stocks in the company William Eldridge had founded; some was in a trust to be transferred to Winifred upon her 21st birthday; and there was, in addition, a joint savings account which was in both Agnes' and Winifred's name. The Bellingham house had been willed to George and Helen with the stipulation that Helen would live there indefinitely, and any sale of the property would have to be by mutual consent.

A sum more than adequate was also left for Winifred to attend the university of her choice. She had the advance acceptance at Wellesley, but she decided that a school with the reputation of the University of Washington would meet her undergraduate needs. She could save thousands as a resident student, and use her money for a higher degree. She would then have enough to purchase a car. She asked Mr. Fleming to handle her finances which he was pleased to do. He admired the girl's prudence and maturity.

Winifred invested in a second hand Pontiac that one of the academy's faculty members had owned, and drove to Seattle to take early entrance exams for the University of Washington. Her summer program plus one more semester at St. Ann's had given her sufficient credits for early enrollment. She promised Miss Hopper that if she were accepted at the university, she would return in the spring for commencement ceremonies. She was already the acknowledged valedictorian, and no other student could challenge her.

During the noon break at entrance exams, a tall blonde girl who defined the term "statuesque," approached Winifred. "Hi! Are you a late entry?"

"No, I'm early, actually. I'll finish my academy credits this term and I'd like to enroll here beginning winter quarter."

"Academy—private school?"

"Yes. St. Ann's in Portland."

"You're way ahead of me, then. After high school I took time off to be with with my folks—we're a military family—I spent five years overseas."

"That's an education in itself. Where?" Winifred asked.

"Mostly Germany with side trips to Italy and France. I loved it, but enough was enough. I needed to get back to school before I got too old!"

"How could you be too old? Lots of students have to work before beginning college."

"I know, but I have my heart set on pre-med, and the competition is fierce. There's so much math and science and I can't afford to lag much further behind. By the way, I'm Ruth Bentley."

"Winifred Effinger."

"Winnie, I presume—or Freddie?"

Winifred laughed. "I was raised by my grandmother and aunt.

Aunt Helen wouldn't allow me to be called 'Winnie.' She said it sounded like what a horse does when it's hungry!"

"And Freddie?"

"That never came up, but I'm sure my aunt would have had some objection."

The girls ate lunch in the commons and exchanged biographical details. They discovered they had many similar interests. The subject of housing came up.

"Are you going to live in a dorm or a sorority?" Ruth asked.

"I plan to live in a dorm. I'm definitely not the Greek Row type."

"Why not? You're just what some houses need, a great looker with high grades from an elite private academy."

Winifred laughed. "Good looking? If I were you, I wouldn't be worried about catching up on science and math, I'd get to an eye doctor and have your glasses changed!" Ruth wore glasses with dark frames which set off her light hair and yet did not dim her bright hazel eyes.

"Oh, bosh. You're an attractive girl. I'll bet your hair is naturally wavy! I have to put mine up in curlers every night or I'm a disaster." She tilted her head scrutinizing Winifred and paused before she remarked, "If you used just a trace of lipstick, and not pull your hair back so severely you'd be a real knock out! Take it on my authority; the boys will be standing in line."

"They'll have a long wait," Winifred said. It was time to change the subject. "What about you? —Sorority or dorm?"

"Dorm? No, thank God. My Aunt Irene has a huge house near lower campus. She didn't want to give it up when my uncle died, so she turned it into a boarding house. She's happy as a mouse in a cheese factory to cook and mother her set of residents."

"I love your imagery!" Winifred said.

"Say," Ruth began, "what if Aunt Irene had room for you? Would you be interested? "

"Sure."

"You'll have to meet each other, of course."

Ruth had planned to take the city bus to Montlake where her aunt's house overlooked Lake Washington and the university arboretum. Instead, Winifred drove them. Irene Bentley was a handsome woman in her fifties. She was tall, like her niece, with graying hair, but a youthful face. After an hour of visiting, she invited Winifred to stay to dinner. "If you decide to be a part of our family—I call my boarders that with great affection—you will need to sample the menu."

"You would have room for me?" Winifred asked.

"I certainly would. In fact, you'd have a choice of rooms. There's a large one upstairs that is sunny with a view of Lake Washington and the arboretum. The other space is in the basement. It's not fancy, but you'd have your own bathroom. There's an adjoining room and no one else downstairs. Your typewriter wouldn't disturb anyone."

The "basement" was warm and spacious with a sliding glass patio door that connected to the garden. Mrs. Bentley promised that she would provide a desk as well as a dresser and bed. "This is what the British maiden ladies would call a bed sitting room American style. I have one rule: no male visitors in rooms, but there is free use of the parlor, and I'm always happy to welcome an occasional guest at our dinner table. Are you interested?"

"Oh yes, please!" Winifred said enthusiastically.

"Aunt Irene has me in the attic so my typewriter won't be heard either," Ruth said.

After dinner, which reminded Winifred of her grandmother's cooking, she and Mrs. Bentley settled details of move in time, and compensation. She would return within a few weeks after completing her requirements at the academy.

Leaving St. Ann's, both students and faculty wished Winifred well and Miss Hopper pointed out that this was not a good bye, but the farewell to adolescence and the beginning of her adult life.

"Have you decided on a major?" Miss Harris asked.

"English literature, thanks to you!" Winifred replied without hesitation.

"Not journalism? Miss Walker may be disappointed."

"I've thought it through," Winifred replied. "I was all set to major in political science with a minor in journalism, but I believe television news is going to take over from newspapers as a source of information. I can't see myself as a television commentator. My skills are in writing ideas, not in public speaking or performing. And then you got me all fired up about Shakespeare!"

Miss Hopper who had heard the conversation said to Miss Harris, "Now that is a tribute you can treasure."

Her car packed with personal belongings, Winifred began the drive north with optimism. She believed that the loose ends of her life were knitting together for the first time since she had left Bellingham High School.

Winter quarter then spring passed quickly. Winifred had kept her promise to speak at St. Ann's commencement exercises. Aunt Helen did not attend, and the Park Department had sent George to Acadia in Maine for the summer. Mrs. Bentley, Ruth and a few of the boarders came to Portland as a gesture of their affection and respect. Ruth passed Biology easily, and was making high marks in math courses, but she had a hard time in written communication skills. Winifred helped her with English requirements, and discovered she liked tutoring. In spite of widely different academic fields, the girls became close friends and constant companions. Aunt Irene scolded them with good humor, but with some seriousness. "Where are the handsome lads I had hoped you girls would bring to Sunday dinner?"

Ruth was quick to reply. "I have too hard a time competing with persons in pants in pre-med. I don't want to socialize and lose any advantage!"

For Winifred's part there were few males in the English Department. The men, many of whom were taking advantage of the

G.I. Bill, seemed not to major in English, but chose accounting, business or sports. Other girls gushed over the sports stars, but Ruth despised the "jocks" as she dubbed what she called the Neanderthals in physical education. Winifred's experience with athletes was different, but she didn't openly disagree.

Winifred was happier than she had been in years. She had made good friends at the academy, but now for the first time since her grade school pal, Victoria, she had a relationship in the tradition of the Anne of Green Gable's "bosom friend."

In the summer after their junior year, both young women decided to skip the first half of summer quarter. George and Marion had invited Winifred to come to Flathead Lake repeatedly, and she felt that this was an ideal time. Winifred had not returned to Bellingham since her grandmother's funeral. Aunt Helen had made some attempts to bridge the gap between her niece and herself by correspondence. They had met upon occasion when Helen and Mildred came to Seattle for the theatre or symphony. When Ruth and Winifred joined them for a concert in the spring, Helen took Winifred aside and confided that Mildred had at last separated from Dr. Sutherland. He had pushed his wife too far when he left his receptionist and had a blatantly public affair with a woman decades younger. Mildred settled for a car, stocks, and half interest in the future sale of their house. She signed off on the yacht, and agreed to a modest alimony. The divorce was settled with the satisfaction of both parties.

The news took a weight from Winifred's concern for her aunt. Since Grandmother's death she had felt a niggling guilt when she made excuses not to visit Bellingham. Winifred sympathized with the fact that Helen might be lonely. Now that Mildred was free and planning to live with Helen, she saw a difference in her aunt. All through the years of her growing up, Helen had shown generosity in many ways. She read to Winifred, took her riding, and bought her books. But it was from her grandmother that she received hugs, and the signs of affection which showed love in non material ways. Remembering

Grandmother's face, Winifred recalled smiles; the image of Aunt Helen always seemed serious and remote. The evening when Helen told her of Mildred's divorce, she saw for the first time what she could describe as happiness. Winifred wrote to her aunt telling her that she was going to Montana to visit George and Marion, but she promised that before the next half of summer term, she would visit her and Mildred in Bellingham. If they had time after their trip, she hoped that Ruth would come along. It was important to her that her friend would know where she had grown up.

Ruth and Winifred set out for a leisurely drive to Montana in a roundabout route via the beaches on the Washington coast. They drove from the coast to Portland, stopped to pay respects to Elizabeth Hopper and then east via the mountains of Idaho. They chose picnic spots in state parks and scenic detours along the way where they cooked meat and hot dogs on a small *hibachi*. Ruth had tried to convince Winifred that it would be great fun to purchase a tent and camping equipment, but when Winifred told George and Marion that this was what they might do, George was swift to discourage the plan.

"It's not prudent for two girls alone to camp out in places where you could come to harm."

Winifred had agreed to Ruth's disappointment.

They had been enroute for a week when it seemed they would either have to drive on or spend an uncomfortable night in their car. For miles in Montana there were few motels, and the places that had space seemed to be run down flea traps. Finally in Missoula they found accommodations. They were exhausted after twelve straight hours of driving, and had dinner in the coffee shop before falling into bed for the night.

Winifred awoke from a deep sleep feeling Ruth's hand stroking her hair. Winifred feigned sleep, not knowing quite how to handle her reaction to this overture of affection. The fondling was not offensive; it seemed natural. She turned to Ruth who had nestled close. Winifred let her know that she had awakened. Hesitantly lips met and they kissed, as Winifred thought, "sweetly," thinking of Shakespeare's lines. They remained in each other's arms until first light. They got up, prepared for the drive ahead, and said little to each other, but Ruth reached out to hold Winifred's hands as she took her turn driving. They delayed their arrival in Kalispel by seeing the sights in Glacier and clinging to their time alone. They had been the closest of friends. Before they reached George and Marion's home, they were lovers.

Marion insisted upon giving the girls separate rooms, and there was no logical reason to protest.

"I miss you," Ruth whispered to Winifred at breakfast the first day.

"Me too!" Winifred didn't confess that she had cried at the separation until her pillow was damp.

On the way home they talked about the next year. "Why don't we get an apartment of our own?" Winifred proposed.

"I can't afford that, and what would we tell Aunt Irene?"

When they returned to the boarding house, the matter was settled for them. Irene asked the girls if they would have any objection to sharing a room. A dear friend of hers had recently lost her husband and had been forced to sell her home. Irene had invited her to her home.

"I know it would be inconvenient for you girls, but I'd make it up to you by giving you the room Mrs. Greguson occupied which is larger and, as you know, has a wonderful view."

"But what about the noise of our typewriters?" Winifred asked.

"Don't worry. The adjoining room is where I have my sewing machine and I use it for general storage. I don't think my occasional sewing would bother you!"

Ruth and Winifred assured her that they wouldn't mind.

"Good! Then I will call Vera and tell her all is arranged."

The girls were discreet and took care not to give any indication of a relationship other than good friends in the tradition of sharing a dorm room. Their senior year was happy. Winifred couldn't imagine what life without Ruth would mean to her. She gave no thought to future separation. Ruth would be in medical school at the University of Washington and Winifred had already been accepted for her combined masters and doctoral studies. With a view to helping Ruth through medical school, she had accumulated the credits required for a state teaching certificate. During one quarter she completed student teaching after which the placement secretary for the Department of Education told her she could almost guarantee that Winifred would be hired anywhere she applied.

Winifred came home one afternoon to find Ruth in tears. "I didn't make U.W. medical school," she sobbed.

"What happened?" Winifred asked, shocked. "You're at the top of your class!"

"It seems there are quotas," Ruth explained, blowing her nose "Having been through pre-med here isn't an advantage."

"What will we do?" Winifred asked sitting on the bed and putting her arms around Ruth. "You had your heart set on medical school."

"I still do. That hasn't changed." Ruth's tears had stopped. "I've been accepted at Cornell and at the University of Chicago. I have to pick one or the other, and I guess I'd prefer Ithaca to Chicago."

"You didn't tell me that you had applied to other schools—I could apply at Cornell," Winifred said brightening. "Having been elected to Phi Beta Kappa won't hurt, and it might be good to continue at another university, and I could teach anywhere!"

Ruth shook her head. "No. That wouldn't be good. Living here while in med school is one thing, but even here we'd be in totally different tracks not to mention schedules. I'd never have time for us and we have to face that fact wherever we were. It's better all the way around for me to move and for you to stay here, at least for now."

They talked half the night. Winifred promised to visit Ithaca every vacation. She could afford the travel because of her grandmother's bequest. They promised each other to write often and talk over the telephone. It wouldn't be the same as living together, but until both had completed the education they needed for their future, it was all they could do.

Winifred had another idea. "Let's go to Europe this summer! I can afford to pay for both of us. It could be a last fling before I have to concentrate on passing my orals!"

Ruth wouldn't agree. "There won't be time. I have to leave in three weeks." They should, as Ruth advised, "put on a good face" so as not to provoke gossip about their relationship.

Winifred had never given a thought to gossip. Certainly she and Ruth had been prudent. Although they had twin beds they slept together, alternating so it would seem they slept apart. What Winifred did not suspect was that Ruth had begun to feel trapped by the situation. She knew how hurt Winifred would be if she learned that when she stayed late for "meetings" or laboratory work, in reality she went out with her fellow students. Ruth chaffed at the restrictions her relationship with Winifred imposed. She began to plot a means of separation, and the perfect one would be medical school at another institution. She told Winifred she had applied to the University of Washington, but she had not.

Winifred was heartbroken when Ruth left for Cornell. Ruth was far more self possessed, and told Winifred that this was probably because she was older. "You're still so very young," which was a patronizing remark. Winifred interpreted it as a sign of Ruth's loving concern. She counted the months then weeks until she would fly to Ithaca to spend Christmas with Ruth.

When Christmas approached, Ruth called to tell her that they couldn't be together as planned. "Dad is retiring from active service, and he and my mom have bought a home not far from here. It's a very small place—they want me to be with them for the holidays even though I'll be sleeping on the couch. I can't possibly turn them down."

There was nothing Winifred could do but accept the situation. She buried her emotions and disappointments in her work. Another year passed. Ruth found reasons not to leave New York, and to discourage Winifred's visits. After Winifred was awarded her Masters degree, advisors had urged her to skip the thesis and begin work toward her

PhD. This was a challenge and a distraction. Her advisor summoned her to discuss the quality of her achievements and the subject she chose for her future dissertation. They recommended that she apply for a fellowship to study abroad, but she hadn't acted on their advice. Elizabeth Hopper was a voice Winifred had listened to from the time of her academy days. When she sought her advice, Miss Hopper was at a loss to understand what was holding her former student back. She assumed that it might be a long overdue wish to reestablish family ties with her aunt, but nevertheless counseled Winifred to apply for a grant, so that all her options would be open.

"If you believe you shouldn't go abroad at this time," Miss Hopper told her, "then you may refuse the honor should it be offered to you. At least you will have a choice."

Winifred accelerated her studies and earned the praise of her professors. She applied to take the oral examinations for her doctorate. If she passed, it would mean she had jumped a high hurdle on her way to a PhD. She would have several years to complete her dissertation, and what better place than in Ithaca with Ruth? She would be with her soul mate. The day received her transcript of grades, she received a formal offer of a Fulbright grant to Oxford University. The Fulbright grant in hand, she would call Ruth and discuss a new plan. For years Winifred had looked forward to a summer in Europe. Each year Ruth had discouraged the possibility advising Winifred to stay at the University of Washington to prepare for her orals. "Don't lose a precious summer," she'd said. Now it appeared that there didn't need to be a choice between joining Ruth and continuing her academic work: she could do both. She left the university early enough to call Ruth.

When Winifred walked in the door eager to talk to call New York, the unanticipated blow fell. "Oh, my dear!" Irene gushed. "You just missed Ruth's call! Isn't it all wonderful? Shame on you! How could you have kept this a secret?"

"A secret?"

"You little deceiver," Irene teased smiling broadly. "But I do understand how you would want me to hear the news from Ruth herself. The wedding will be here in Harold's hometown, and I'm sure you'll be the maid of honor! Oh, isn't this just the most welcome news?"

Winifred controlled her emotions with a fierce act of will. "Well, I guess the cat's out of the bag. When are they coming west?" She fixed a smile on her face and hoped she would maintain control."

"Next week! I'm so excited!"

Winifred's expression sobered. "But that's terrible news for me. Look what came in today's mail." She flashed the announcement of her Fulbright grant, but took it back before Irene read the date which was a month away. "I have my passport ready, and I'll have to leave soon—tomorrow, if I want to see my Aunt Helen before I go."

"Oh dear, but you'll call Ruth right away, won't you?" Irene asked.

"Yes, of course." But to herself she added, *when hell hits 30 below zero.*

Irene took Winifred's news in stride. She could not discount the honor of the fellowship, and such things were not to be postponed. "I hate to see you leave, and so suddenly, Winifred. You're a part of my little family."

"I won't be home for dinner, Mrs. Bentley, I have a meeting on campus." Winifred made a swift exit to her car. Tears blinded her eyes and she pulled into a parking place near the stadium on the north side of the ship canal bridge. There she sobbed uncontrollably until daylight began to fade. An instinct of self preservation impelled her to gather her shattered emotions and drive to the Northgate Mall where she found a storage facility which advertised packing boxes. She purchased several and also cushioning material and tape. Then she started back to the boarding house via Greenlake where she parked until it was late enough for Irene to have retired.

She drove through the alley to the back entrance of Irene's home, and carried her boxes upstairs to her room. She put clothes appropriate for her journey overseas into a large suitcase. The rest she packed in boxes to leave in Bellingham. Wrapping gifts from Ruth which she had treasured, she bound that box securely and labeled it to be donated to the Salvation Army. She made several trips to her car with books, and finally with her typewriter. After cleaning the room thoroughly, she sat at her desk to compose a note to Irene Bentley. She doubted her ability to keep her self control if she had to face the woman again. Her note apologized for her unceremonious departure. Under the circumstances there was no time for proper goodbyes. She expressed her appreciation and left the letter in front of Irene's door with a check for the month's board. She slipped out of the house before dawn.

She parked at Greenlake again until mid morning when she drove down town to the British Air travel offices on 5th Avenue. She bought a ticket for two weeks ahead for a flight which would leave for London from Vancouver, B.C. Helen and Mildred were sure to drive her to the Vancouver airport and she could leave her car and packed boxes with them. Her next stop was the university where she shared the good news with her advisors.

The methodical packing and travel arrangements helped Winifred keep from giving in to despair. Now as she drove north, she was numb. She didn't know how to define how she felt. This hurt was too deep. Betrayal came to mind. Certainly that was part of her pain. There was something else, and it was surprising. She was heart broken, but she was also angry with herself. She felt like a fool. She had made protestations of undying love and accepted the same from Ruth. When had this commitment ceased to have meaning for Ruth? *Why did I trust her*? Winifred asked herself. The answer was simple and uncomplicated: *I loved her.* Obviously Ruth's affection was conditional, or perhaps a better word for it was "temporary."

Exhausted and emotionally drained, Winifred stopped in Everett north of Seattle and checked into a downtown hotel. First she stopped at a liquor store for what she wryly told herself was "Listerine comfort." With a bottle of brandy tucked in her purse, and hauling her suitcase, she registered. Soaking in a hot bath while drinking several glasses of brandy on ice, she emerged wrapped in a towel and sat on the bed propped up by pillows. Color television was the new thing in hotels. Her room had a set. In her liquor clouded mind this seemed like a puzzle that she should be able to solve. How did the mechanics of this process work? Maybe she should have majored in science. She continued to watch programs which had no interest to her, poured more brandy and at last fell asleep, the television set still on.

The light coming through the windows where she had left the drapes open awakened her and for a moment she couldn't remember just where she was. Stumbling out of bed, she fell to her knees and experienced the effects of her first hangover. Her mouth felt as if she had swallowed a truck load of sand, and her head throbbed to the point she thought her skull would blow open. Unable to stand, she half crawled to the bathroom, the victim of dry heaves. There had been nothing in her stomach to throw up.

She called the front desk and managed to say that she was going to keep the room for another night and that she did not want to be disturbed. She lurched to the door to put the "do not disturb" card on the outside for good measure. She could barely keep her balance. "Christ Jesus!" she gasped, and it was not a prayer.

By late afternoon she began to feel human, and was vowing that her drinking days were over. She could not imagine a state of mental despair that would compel her to take alcohol as a remedy again. Sensibly she removed the do not disturb sign. Then she phoned in an ordered of steak and baked potato from room service with a pitcher of ice water. When she was certain the food would stay settled in her digestive system, she fell back into bed and slept until morning.

Assured that her reflexes were normal, and using real medicinal mouthwash to erase any possible breath of liquor, she dressed, checked out, and drove the rest of the way to Bellingham. Mildred and Helen greeted her warmly and were thrilled when she told them of her grant. Aunt Helen's delight was sincere. Winifred realized that the last vestiges of her resentment toward her aunt had fallen away.

"My dear," Mildred said with concern, "you are so thin! I hope you'll allow yourself some extra time to relax and enjoy yourself before you take on serious work."

It was true that Winifred's clothes hung noticeably loose. It was mostly because the years of missing Ruth had taken away her appetite. She hadn't minded losing extra pounds, but she was far from "thin." She had never been obsessed with her weight or prone to go on crash diets. Ruth had made her aware that appearances could be important in a professional career and had helped her choose suitable and tasteful outfits, especially when Winifred had done her student teaching. Ruth had always been concerned with her own appearance, and the result was that she looked "put together" as she would say. The only time Winifred could claim such was when she had competed in horse shows years before under the tutelage of Aunt Helen. The trim jodhpurs, polished boots, and tailored riding jacket complimented Winifred's tall frame. Helen had pulled back her long hair and neatly encased it in a net. At St. Ann's Winifred had worn the ensemble complete with riding crop, helmet, and starched white blouse as a Halloween costume. Her friends had teased her: "Where's the horse?"

Mildred continued with her particular advice: "You should buy yourself some sturdy English tweeds over there. Stop in London and go to Harrods," she urged.

"I'll do that," Winifred promised.

Winifred had a window seat on the aircraft leaving from Vancouver flying over the pole. She was relieved to discover that she was alone in her row. She had exhausted her strength of will during her Bellingham stay and was in no mood for casual conversation. It had not been easy to conceal her deep sense of loss and betrayal from Helen and Mildred.

Once past the Northwest Territory she saw a vast expanse of ice below. The sun glowed orange gold on the horizon, and never seemed to set. Winifred thought to herself that it seemed like dawn rather than sunset all day. She put her head on the small pillow, not to sleep but to close her eyes for a bit. Before long, lulled by the sound of the engine and the darkened cabin, she drifted into sleep.

When she awoke she saw the edge of the ice fields below and water. A tiny image of a boat left a white thread of its wake behind. The land appeared bleak without vegetation. When an attendant passed she asked, "Where are we?"

"We're approaching northern Scotland."

Within the hour the pilot announced that he was beginning a descent and soon the plane was in thick clouds. There was no break until the craft broke through immediately before landing. Rows of red roof houses set in neat rows appeared on the outskirts of the tarmac.

On the ground Winifred passed through customs quickly. The official asked her for her destination and reason for the visit.

"I'm here on a fellowship to Oxford, Sir."

"Jolly good," he said affably. He gave her wide smile "Good luck to you."

Outside she hailed a cab. "Kensington East Hotel, please." The driver was an Indian with a white headdress. He was friendly and asked her if she were in London for a vacation. When she told him she would be going up to Oxford, but that she wanted to see some of London first, he reached back to her with a tourist folder and a subway schedule.

"You'll find an underground entry close to your hotel just around the corner from Boots." He spoke with a lilting accent.

"Boots?"

"The chemist. I believe you call it a drug store in America."

In spite of the thirteen hour flight, Winifred was wide awake. She thought she must have slept for at least seven hours. *There's something to be said for emotional exhaustion,* she thought. When she was settled in her hotel room, she decided to visit Harrods. The subway directions and tourist guides were clear, and she had no trouble finding the famous department store. She stopped on several floors, and sat down in a cafeteria for a coffee and scone. She said "yes" when the waitress asked her if she wished clotted cream even though she hadn't the slightest idea what it was. *Why not be adventuresome?* She thought.

Out of curiosity she went to the equestrian department where the display of saddles and tack was impressive and very expensive. The smell of good leather reminded her of Mildred and that she had promised to buy warm clothes. By the time she had made her purchases she was feeling the effects of jet lag. Returning to Kensington East with some crusty bread and white cheddar cheese from Harrod's bakery for a supper, she undressed and fell into bed. She was soon asleep.

The next day she felt rested and ready to see London. On a famous two tiered tourist bus she acquired an overview of the city, and then used her underground guide to visit Trafalgar Square where she saw a formal changing of the Queen's guard complete with scarlet helmet guards on black horses. For the evening she bought a ticket to a concert at St. Martin of the Fields, and a tour to Stratford on Avon for the following day.

In Stratford she was enchanted by the white swans on the river. After seeing Anne Hathaway's cottage, she bought a postcard and sent a note to Helen and Mildred. "The Elizabethans must have been very short," she wrote, "I had to duck to pass from room to room!"

The replica of the Globe, and especially the performance of *A Winter's Tale* which was rarely seen at home, was impressive. She had seen Shakespeare performed when Katharine Hepburn's production of *As You Like It* came to Seattle. She had loved Olivier's *Henry V* and the old movie version of *Midsummer Night's Dream*. But none of these could compare with the Globe performance of the bard's plays as they had been staged in Shakespeare's time. She fought the recurrence of tears when she remembered how she had looked forward to sharing the experience with Ruth.

When she returned to London, a call to her contact at Oxford confirmed that her room was ready, and she was welcome to arrive at any time. She wasted no time, and took the train north by the next morning. The week she planned to spend as a tourist in London was not lifting her spirits; instead she thought how sterile solitude was without Ruth. She needed to immerse herself in work.

The first year at Oxford helped Winifred deal with the wounds of Ruth's rejection, but the healing was slow. Among her peers, Winifred appeared friendly but reserved. She conversed with ease, and gave the impression of a well adjusted young woman. That was the external Winifred Eldridge. The inner person, the core of her, remained hidden. She told herself that she would spin a cocoon, a place hidden and safe from further injury. An impenetrable encasement would be her protection.

Her state of mind did not affect her brilliant academic achievement. Her dissertation research was taking shape. In a world literature class during her pre graduate days she had discovered Castigleone and his treatise on "Courtly Love." She had immediately drawn comparisons with the tradition in Shakespeare characters such as Orlando and Romeo. Other parallels were striking and her research was directed to making a case that Shakespeare may have known of and used Castigleone's ideas. She feared that her Oxford advisors and peers would scoff at such a leap of logic, but they did not. One don told her that if she completed the work with the fulfillment of its early promise, it could prove to be as valuable in Shakespearean scholarship as Spenser's *Shakespeare and the Nature of Man.*

By the end of her first year Winifred began to understand her relationship with Ruth. She was able to see herself from the outside looking in. For a span of years she thought her love of Ruth was a life commitment of fidelity; now she realized it was as much like puppy love as Antonio's opening speech in *The Merchant of Venice.* It was an adolescent crush. Her involvement had not resulted in growth for her as a person in her own right. She sat in the park by the river on a warm July day, exactly one year since she had arrived in England. She knew she had progressed in her academic life, but she was stalled in emotional limbo. "Enough!" She said to herself. She had to break the chrysalis and emerge into the light.

On the bulletin board in the building where she had her rooms, there was a note inviting any four of the house residents for a drive through the Cotswolds. "First come, first included," the sign read. The planned destination was the town of Burford, where the group would experience the traditional "high tea" at a local establishment. Winifred put her name on the card. At the appointed place, she met Charles Hastings, a Rhodes scholar, who was driving; Pamela Downing, a young woman from Northwestern University; and Amy Mates, a British citizen from London. She thought to herself that reverting to her pre-Ruth friendly disposition was ironically recapturing the best part of her adolescent years.

Of the three companions Winifred discovered that she had more in common with Charles. He had visited Seattle's World's Fair before flying to England, and had seen the University of Washington campus. His major was political science, and after he completed his year at Oxford, he had hoped to work with President Kennedy's Committee to Re-elect. November of 1963 had dashed his hopes. "When I heard the news I said to myself I'll be damned if I'd work for Johnson," he told Winifred. He had come to England shortly afterwards. Winifred described the mood after the assasination at Oxford when American students were amazed by the reaction not only within the university, but from the town. Large books were place on campus for expressions of sympathy to be sent to the Kennedy family. By 1965 Lyndon Johnson's concept of the Great Society and his advocacy for civil rights had altered Charles' precipitous reaction.

Charles tested some of his dissertation ideas by giving impromptu lectures to Winifred, his "audience of one" as he would say. She grasped more of his content than he did of hers.

"What the hell is this courtly love stuff? Why would anyone spend years on that crap?" Charles asked her one day.

Winifred took the question without antagonism. "We're a strange bunch," she replied, "—those of us in literary criticism. You might say that we're up in our ivory tower, or perpetually peering through Alice's looking glass! But within my world of books, I see views of the human condition that are every bit as relevant to real life as your political theories."

"Point taken," Charles said.

Winifred's friendship with Charles was like having a brother. There was no element of romance, just an easy camaraderie. She was sorry when he left Oxford, but although she missed his company and their good natured banter, it had not been a heart wrenching separation.

After her years in England and a completed dissertation, Winifred returned to Seattle. She had passed her orals before leaving for Europe. Now she would defend her dissertation with the poise and confidence her years at Oxford had given her. She thought with a smile that her arguments with Charles had prepared her well.

At commencement ceremonies in the spring of 1967, Winifred now twenty-eight, accepted the doctoral hood bestowed upon her by the University of Washington. She was now "Dr. Winifred Eldridge." Helen, Mildred, George and Marion were present along with Elizabeth Hopper, faculty from St. Ann's Academy, and a few of her class members.

After the ceremony, Helen hosted a party at the University District's Edmond Meany Hotel. The group called, "Speech! Speech!" Winifred had one ready.

"This day was made possible by many who are here this evening. You all know how dear you are in my regard and gratitude. There is one thing more: I have been offered and have accepted a position as an assistant professor at the University of Washington."

The room exploded with the ring of applause and congratulations.

Helen and Mildred had decided to stay overnight at the hotel after the dinner party, and Winifred left for Portland with Elizabeth Hopper. She had promised to speak at St. Ann's commencement exercises. When Miss Hopper discovered that Winifred would be driving alone, she had asked if she could ride with her. "Miss Tate's car is full considering she and Miss Harris brought several of the alumni you invited—if I wouldn't be intruding?"

"Not at all! I'd be happy to have the company," Winifred assured her.

"Have you given thought to where you'll live in Seattle?" Miss Hopper asked when they were on the road south.

"I'm going to look for an apartment close to campus. Summer's probably a good time to find something. If I have to stay in a dorm room until something turns up, that's all right with me."

"May I be what is called a 'butt-in-ski?'" Miss Hopper questioned.

"Butt in all you like!" Winifred laughed.

"I have a friend who teaches in the Drama department at the university. Perhaps you met her?—Aristelle Arnold?"

"No, I don't recall, and I'm sure I'd remember that name."

"She teaches drama and also directs. This summer she's involved with the off campus repertory theatre's *Tug Boat Annie.*"

"Acting or directing? Don't tell me she's Annie!"

"She is. She's a talented lady. I met her through Kappa Alpha Gamma, the educational honorary. One summer we were in a group attending the Ashland Shakespeare festival and I shared a hotel room with her. We've been friends ever since. She lives in a large house just on the other side of Greek Row. Her daughter and son-in-law have been pressuring her to let them share her house which would mean that instead of ruling her own roost, Aristelle would be hardly more than a boarder. She's looking for someone to share expenses, but had almost given up."

"I take it your friend isn't on the best of terms with the daughter and son-in-law?"

"No, she isn't. Greg and Gail are "born again" Christians. I don't mean to cover that whole group under one blanket, but they are two of the most intolerant individuals I've ever encountered."

"You've met them?"

"During a conference last year I stayed with Aristelle—the house is huge, plenty of room for guests. I joined Gail and Greg for dinner and had to listen to Greg's ranting about the evils of homosexuality and liberal politicians. Gail had hated Kennedy, and didn't have any use for Lyndon Johnson and his civil rights policies. Dinner conversation was a one sided monologue, and I wondered how Aristelle with her intellect and respect for humanity could ever have produced this daughter. I could call her and arrange a meeting if you'd like. —That is if you wouldn't mind living with someone almost as ancient as I am."

"You're not what I'd call 'ancient,' " Winifred said.

"Perhaps not ancient, but my sixty-two is over the top of that proverbial hill."

"I gather she's a widow?"

"No. Divorced. I don't know all of the circumstances, but I do know that her daughter chose to live with her father." Miss Hopper smiled. "Her colleagues at the university have a rhyme: 'Is she in heaven, or is she in hell?—That damned unpredictable Aristelle!' She's famous in drama circles. Her ability to direct is legendary. She also inspires her student actors to penetrate their characters' motivations and in the process understand their own."

"I might be interested. It depends on what she would expect of me. I value my privacy and I'm not the most sociable of individuals."

"I'll call her."

Winifred found the address Aristelle Arnold gave her. It was a large house set back from the tree lined street. There were winding stairs going up to the main entrance which was flanked by flowering shrubs. There appeared to be a basement as well as a second story. The front yard was perfectly maintained with bushes of heather, Rhododendrons, a rose garden, and containers of vivid blue trailing lobelia cascading over the porch railing. Winifred rang the doorbell. She heard music within and was about to ring a second time when Aristelle opened the door.

"Dr. Eldridge, I presume? Come in. I was just about to make tea, unless you would prefer coffee?"

"Tea is fine, thank you."

Aristelle ushered Winifred into the living room which was a beautifully appointed parlor. She could see a library on the left of the hall, and opening from the living room, a dining area with a table that could easily seat a dozen people. For one heart stopping moment Winifred wondered if this had become a boarding house and if so, she'd manage to retreat as quickly as the demands of courtesy would allow.

Aristelle returned with a tray. There were two china cups, sugar, milk and lemon and a dish of shortbread wafers. It reminded Winifred of Grandmother's hospitality, but there the similarity ended. Grandmother was petite and reserved while Aristelle was a large and expansive presence. If this woman walked on stage, Winifred thought, all eyes would be drawn to her, and yet up close she didn't seem to demand attention either by her voice or movements. Winifred had some trouble concentrating on the content of Aristelle's conversation. Her voice was low and melodious with a timbre similar to actress Judith Anderson's. *What an experience it would be to hear this woman read Shakespeare's sonnets or Walt Whitman's poetry,* she thought. She forced herself to pay attention.

After they had their tea, Aristelle took Winifred on a tour of the house. "I live in the bedroom down on this floor," she said, "I find that with the weight of years plus pounds, the second floor is not convenient. This house is too big for one person, but it would break my heart to leave it." There was an alcove with an upright piano, the room devoted to posters and memorabilia of years of theatrical productions. She led the way upstairs. "Up here there are three bedrooms, a complete bath and a shower adjoining the back bedroom. Were you to consider living here, you would have the entire second floor to yourself. You've seen the downstairs. In the cold months I almost always have a fire in the fireplace in the evening and settle in my much too comfortable recliner to read. A brisk after dinner walk would be healthier, but my body is lazy while my brain works overtime!"

Winifred was drawn to this woman. She could characterize her as an "earth mother" type, but not entirely. She didn't patronize or mother Winifred. She was business like, and at the same time warm and friendly. She did not reach out as Irene Bentley had done metaphorically gathering her boarders into welcoming arms.

"The kitchen would be yours as much as mine, but I hope that sometimes you might want to share a meal. I love to cook, which won't surprise you considering my size!"

Aristelle was neither fat nor flabby, but she was, how would Winifred characterize it? "Ample" came to mind. She was also a very handsome woman. Her thick, white hair was beautifully coiffed— more than likely at a weekly beauty parlor session. Her black eyebrows in contrast, was evidence that she had been a raven haired beauty in her youth. She had even teeth, obviously her own, and smiled easily with her gray eyes as well as her mouth. Rimless glasses did not detract from the warmth of her expression.

Aristelle took Winifred down to the basement which was clean and mostly empty. "My friends up at Denny Hall tell me this would be an enviable wine cellar, but I've never been that much of a wine gourmet. To tell you the truth, I'm satisfied with Gallo with a screw on top, and God forgive me, Manichewitz! I don't even own a corkscrew." Her eyes fairly sparkled. "If that is a deal breaker, say so and I will go out and invest in some sophisticated brands!"

"By all means, do that!" Winifred countered, and then told her that she was far from a connoisseur. "I do know something about brandy, however, and then told her about the St. Ann's Listerine bottle." She added hastily—"But you must never tell Elizabeth Hopper!"

"I promise complete silence! I can't imagine, though, that she doesn't know. She has an uncanny ability of keeping track of her girls."

Winifred continued her "confessions," and told her about the boiler room group of which Miss Hopper had known.

They talked about rent which was a ridiculously low figure. "My dear," Aristelle said, I believe you would make the perfect—what shall I say?—guest, companion, boarder, not to mention friend. I'm not teaching summer session, but I'll have late rehearsals for a production at the Rep. You'll be on your own, and I wouldn't be around to keep you company."

"I'm noted for being a hermit. Aside from a few beer parties with fifty or sixty of my rowdy friends, I'll be content," Winifred said playfully.

Part Three

From her front window Aristelle watched Winifred until her car had disappeared down the boulevard. She had resisted the practicality of sharing her home until Elizabeth Hopper called recommending this young woman. She trusted her friend's judgment. The timing was fortuitous. Property taxes would be due shortly after the fall quarter began. This, as well as the expense of keeping up the garden and maintaining the house, made the decision an imperative rather than a choice.

After pouring another cup of tea, Aristelle settled in her recliner. The fire and a table lamp was all the light she needed, and she settled back with the scripts she was considering for coming productions. As she opened Ibsen's *The Doll's House*, she let her thoughts wander back to September, 1941. Memories came to mind with vivid clarity. She had chided herself that day for her colossal nerve. How could a sophomore history major with no stage experience have the nerve to try out for a play at UCLA? There would probably be fifty other females hoping to play Nora in Ibsen's *A Doll's House*. When she saw what could be a hundred or more in line outside the audition theatre to register, her courage had almost failed her. As well as her inexperience, this was the first time in her life that she would have defied her father's will. She remembered thinking that bolting would be easier than going through an exercise in futility. Yet, unqualified as she was, she had reasoned that going through the process was a valuable experience in itself. And surely a twenty year old woman should have the courage to stand up to a father's authority—even that of Colonel Garrison Arnold.

When she was a high school student, she would have loved to participate in high school drama, but her father wouldn't hear of it. Also, being the daughter of an army officer meant that no posting was permanent, and if she had gotten a part, there was always the possibility the she would have had to move before a performance. Her sense of fairness told her that accepting a role would not have been honorable even if she could have convinced Colonel Arnold that an extra curricular activity would strengthen an application for university admission. She was eighteen when he was posted to San Francisco, and the family had expected to remain there until retirement. Aristelle managed to win a scholarship to UCLA which paid for her tuition. It had helped to persuade her parents to permit her to attend a school some six hundred miles away.

Aristelle remembered clearly how when she had reached the head of the long line of audition hopefuls, fifty or more students had lined up behind her. One of three drama majors who sat behind a card table gave her a 3 x 5 card with number 134 in bold print. She wrote her name beside the corresponding number on the audition list. *You couldn't call this process overly personal*, she had thought. Considering that this was UCLA, and many aspiring theater majors had the sir names of well known and even famous parents, name recognition would not play a part in first impression. The procedure was fair.

Sitting in her chair by the fire twenty six years later, that day played in Aristelle's mind like one of the scripts she had begun to read. There had been no chairs in the lobby; students sat on the lobby floor, or stood outside waiting for their number to be called. Aristelle had waited for three hours before number 134 was announced. She walked down the theater aisle and climbed the four steps from the orchestra pit to center stage where a reader waited with two scripts.

On the stage a student handed her a script, and the director told her to step closer downstage. "O.K. number 134. Take a look at page 180, the underscored lines."

Preparation time was almost zero as the director continued. "Your husband thinks that women should be submissive, barefoot and pregnant. He has just discovered that you have saved his bacon on your own and he resents it. Kyle, read the cue."

Aristelle had been ignorant of theater jargon. She knew what a cue was, but when she heard the students' conversations as she waited to be called, it was obvious to her that she wasn't in their league. They had debated "the method" which had something to do with a Russian, Stanislavski. She smiled now remembering how in her favor she did have first hand knowledge of a domineering father and the effect he had on her gentle mother. As she read her lines in response to the student reader, the memory of Garrison Arnold's verbal abuse and disrespect rose to the surface. She had read the lines as if it were her mother facing her father. She remembered how she had vowed never to endure the disrespect her mother meekly accepted from him.

Then director had shouted from his place several rows from the stage. "Stop! What's your name?" Aristelle lowered her script, and tried to see who was speaking, but it was difficult because of the light on the stage and the unlit auditorium.

"Aristelle Arnold," she had said. *Was I that bad?* It was too late to bolt now, but she wouldn't need to. The director was about to order her off the stage.

"You've never been through any of my classes." He looked to the woman at his right who shook her head. A bearded man at his left shrugged his shoulders.

He hadn't asked a question, but Aristelle said, "I'm a history major."

The group spoke in almost inaudible tones while Aristelle stood wondering what was being said. She was hearing something of their conversation—enough to believe she had failed her audition. Standing awkwardly she saw that the three still had their heads together.

"Sure, she can read. My God, she's great, but can she move?" Dean Langford asked his colleagues.

"That's the question," the bearded man said, "but calling her back makes sense whether we know her or not. I do have reservations. Most of our kids can read well."

"Oh, I agree, but she didn't just read the part. She lived it even when she was standing up there straight as a stick. She was Nora—heart and soul."

The director had scrutinized her and then thought to himself that she might be too tall. He had always envisioned Nora as small. Also, her hair was not Scandinavian blonde, but crow black.

"O.K., number 134. Please stick around for the next round.

Monday morning after a weekend of grueling final auditions, the cast list was posted on the department's bulletin board. Aristelle was Nora. The final cast met in a classroom where the director discussed his interpretation of the play and the details of rehearsal schedules. Afterwards he asked Aristelle to remain.

"I'm taking a chance with you," he had told her. "However, I've assigned one of our experienced actresses as your understudy. If you prove to be a klutz—or if you even blink in protest to any of my directions, you're out. There are kids in my department who would murder their grandmother for this opportunity. As a matter of fact, I'd watch my back during rehearsals. Some will resent the fact, and rightly, that you haven't paid your dues."

"I'll do my best," Aristelle had said simply.

"Good girl."

It was done. She left the drama building elated, and apprehensive. She was not daunted by the director's warning, but telling her parents that she would have to return to UCLA the Friday after Thanksgiving vacation because she was rehearsing for a play would not be easy. She needed a Lady Macbeth urging her to "screw her courage to the sticking point."

Colonel Arnold had raged and Margaret Arnold, fearing to offend her husband, had tried to persuade her daughter to put family ahead of a frivolous activity. Aristelle had for once held her ground. From his assignment in San Francisco's Presidio, her father couldn't exactly haul her home from Los Angeles by the long arm of the law that prevailed in his household.

Aristelle still remembered that first theatrical role as if it had happened yesterday.

Director Dean Langford had waited in the wings to congratulate his cast and crew for a show well done. *The Doll's House* had run for two weekends; the reviews had come in with far more praise than he expected; and the gate had broken records. He had stopped Aristelle on the way to the girls' dressing room and planted a kiss on her cheek as he enfolded her in a bear hug. "We're doing *Pygmalion* next. Interested?"

Sunday morning following the last performance, Aristelle heard noise out in the dormitory hall. Someone was pounding on the doors up and down the hallway on her floor. "Wake up! We're at war—turn on your radios!"

The mood on campus changed overnight with the news of the war. When students gathered in the common room late in the morning of December 7th, they heard the voice of H.V. Kaltenborn announcing the attack on Pearl Harbor by the Japanese. Life for the young men listening would change, and they knew it. Some were talking about volunteering before their number came up in the draft. The wave of patriotism had a darker side. Students from Japan would be allowed to depart the country, but others, second and third generation Americans, became victims of verbal abuse. Their rooms were vandalized and hate slogans abounded.

War notwithstanding, final examinations were the immediate reality for students. Aristelle had completed hers and was satisfied that her transcript would show that the time spent on the play had not affected her grade point. She was in her dorm room selecting things she wanted to take with her to San Francisco for the winter break when a student knocked on the door calling her to the telephone. It was her mother's voice.

"Are your finals over?" She asked.

"Just this morning. I was packing some things to bring home for Christmas."

"Your father wants you to pack everything."

"Everything? Why?"

"We're being transferred to Fort Lewis in Tacoma, Washington. This is a blessing because he'll be involved in training rather than fighting."

"But Mom, I don't need to go with you. The coming quarter will complete my sophomore year, and…" She hesitated not wanting to confide her prospects in the drama department. "There are other reasons I want to continue here."

"Your father has decided…"

Aristelle had sat on her bed disappointed and angry. She could rebel. But she had reflected that the most compelling argument for complying with her father's demands was her mother. Even as a young girl, Aristelle had realized how demeaning marriage to Garrison Arnold had been for Margaret Arnold. She had endured the humiliation of constant submission. He controlled everything from how she styled her hair to what she should buy in the commissary, and what she cooked for meals. But was it humiliating to her mother? She had been raised in a military family, and was repeating a pattern she never questioned.

By the end of January of 1942 the family was settled in Fort Lewis, and she had met her father's adjutant, Judson Morgan…

Aristelle returned to the present abruptly. "No!" She said aloud. She had no intention of reliving the next eleven years: the desperate unhappiness, and the hopeless entrapment that had been the result of one brief moment of sexual encounter. *I have better things to think about*, she chided herself, and opened Steven Vincent Benet's *John Brown's Body* which she was considering as a production in Readers Theater form.

Winifred's new living arrangement proved to be more than satisfactory. As the weeks of summer passed, it was a happy circumstance for both that she and Aristelle were remarkably compatible. During rehearsal evenings, Winifred had the house to herself and enjoyed her time alone. At the same time she looked forward to Aristelle's company and the anecdotes she brought home from the theatre. *Tugboat Annie* was a success and ran for three weeks. Elizabeth Hopper drove to Seattle to see a performance. Aristelle told Winifred that the third bedroom with the shower bath was hers for guests if she wished, and Elizabeth had enjoyed their hospitality. Helen and Mildred stayed with Winifred when they came to Seattle for an evening at the theatre. Aristelle charmed both ladies. One evening when they visited, Winifred had prevailed upon Aristelle to read from *John Brown's Body* which she was to direct in the spring.

When *Tug Boat Annie* concluded its performances, Aristelle planned to visit her daughter, Gail, in Spokane. Aristelle had referred to her ex-husband and daughter without much explanation. Winifred didn't press for information. Aside from remarks from the theatre people and Elizabeth Hopper, she understood little about the "unpredictable Aristelle" before she had became a professor in the drama department at the university.

Once a year Aristelle made the trip across the mountains to the "Inland Empire" where Gail and her husband Greg had settled. She always stayed at the Davenport Hotel rather than in her daughter's home. Gail had produced no children, and had become passionately religious and increasingly critical of her mother's lack of religion.

Winifred had not yet met Gail, but she did have a brief encounter with Greg. He dropped in unannounced when Aristelle was still at school one afternoon. Recognizing him from pictures, Winifred offered him coffee while he waited for Aristelle. She found the man oddly hostile.

"Wouldn't you rather live independently in your own apartment?" he asked.

"No, to be truthful. Aristelle and I have different schedules and I have all the privacy and independence of my own apartment, but with the advantage of this beautiful home."

"I can understand that," he said. "Aren't you offended by some of her associates?"

"Excuse me?"

"Those commies and queers in drama and speech. You're in another field aren't you?"

"The English Department, yes."

"So your associates are normal?"

The conversation annoyed Winifred. She tried to make her answer light and non confrontational. Laughing she told Greg, "We have some definitely eccentric professors in my department, and they would probably object to being called 'normal.' "

Later when Aristelle said that she would be visiting Gail and Greg in Spokane, Winifred recalled her brief conversation with Greg and was relieved that Aristelle would be going to visit the couple in September before fall session rather than having them invade their home in Seattle. "I'll spend two weeks mainly to keep Gail from complaining I never spend time with them."

Winifred planned to surprise Aristelle while she was away by turning the kitchen into a home canning factory. She had commented several times that she would be sorry to see an end to summer as she hated tinned fruit. "What about home canned?" Winifred had asked.

"Don't I wish!" Aristelle replied. "But I have neither the time nor the skill to put up a supply!"

Winifred had the time, and thanks to Grandmother, the skill. When summer session ended, she drove Aristelle to the Greyhound bus depot. "Try to rest on the way," she told her. "You haven't had a moment to yourself since the last play."

"Sweet Winifred! Who appointed you Mother Hen? I'll be fine," she said smiling. It was a new experience for the "unpredictable" Aristelle to have anyone concerned for her well being. "And don't you burn the midnight oil. "Winifred watched Aristelle's bus roll out of the depot and then headed for the Pike Place Market. She was early enough to grab a decent parking place which she would need considering the heavy load she would be purchasing. She bought boxes of pears, apricots and peaches which came directly from Yakima east of the mountains. These items stored in the trunk of her car, she stopped at the grocery store for canning supplies. Aristelle's kitchen was well appointed, but there was nothing suitable for putting up fruit.

At home she parked in the alley so that she could carry the boxes into the house and avoid the front stairs. Apron on, supplies and fruit organized, she began her project. She had considered canning some wax beans, but that would have involved a pressure cooker and more experience than she had. She surely didn't want her surprise to result in botulism poisoning!

Winifred spent several days peeling, par-boiling, and transferring the fruit into scalding hot jars. She surveyed the result of her work, rows of gleaming jars filled with shades of orange, gold and winter white. She would bring them to the basement where she had purchased a cabinet for storage. The clock in the kitchen read 4:30 in the afternoon, and she was exhausted. She was removing her apron when the phone rang.

"Hello."

"And 'hello' to you, too!"

The voice was familiar, but she couldn't place the caller. It wasn't Aristelle or anyone from the English Department.

"It's me, Ruth, a voice from your past."

A wave of recognition hit Winifred with tsunami force. "Ruth…it's been a long time." It had been nine years. "How are you?" she asked politely but without the enthusiasm of greeting an old friend.

"Good enough. I'm here in Seattle, at Aunt Irene's. She tells me that congratulations are in order, Dr. Eldridge."

"Thank you." Silence. "Are you in residency here?"

"I wish. No. I couldn't stand the pressure."

"You mean you left to get married."

"No, and yes. I couldn't compete with the eastern seaboard crowd. When Harold pressured me to marry him, it was a good out."

Winifred was not prepared for the level of self deprecation from the ever confident Ruth.

"At any rate," Ruth continued, "I'm here with Irene until my divorce goes through."

Another shock. Irene had gushed that Ruth's Prince Charming would ride off into a land of married bliss carrying her to live forever after in the castle of any girl's dreams. So much for romance.

"I'm sorry."

"Well, he decided we were incompatible, but that was because the kids he wanted hadn't started to come in the numbers he anticipated."

"So you didn't have children?"

"One. Harold has custody. I hate to tell you all this on the phone. Can we have dinner tonight? Let's go somewhere spiffy like the Four Seasons down town."

"That would be interesting. What time?"

"Eight?"

Winifred had three hours to come up with an outfit to fit the adjective "spiffy." She searched her closet and found the long black dress she had worn to the party Helen had hosted for her PhD. It had a beaded top, but no appropriate jacket, and it was chilly. Then she remembered Aristelle's grey shawl which was dressy and also beaded. She was certain Aristelle wouldn't mind if she borrowed it. But shoes? There was time for her to drive to the Bon Marche in the north end mall. She bought patent leather pumps with a higher heel than she had ever worn. *I'll never forgive myself for this display of vanity if I fall flat on my face,* she thought. She had taken the liberty of searching Aristelle's jewelry case and found pearl earrings that would match her own string of pearls which Grandmother had given her. As she surveyed the total effect in the full length hall mirror, she realized her hair was a problem. Aristelle to the rescue again. Winifred had let her hair grow long so she could tie it back and not have to fuss with it. She twisted it into a French roll and secured it with two of her friend's combs.

"Well, ugly duckling," she said aloud to her mirror image, "I guess I should try a little make up, as if that would complete my transformation into a swan!" Winifred's self confidence in the academic world had never extended to how she viewed herself. She would have been incredulous if she had heard the way some of her students admired her appearance. Tall and slender with her dark hair pulled back, her blue eyes and full lashes were dominant; so much so the fact that she wore no makeup was unimportant. An art major taking a required English credit had whispered to her companion, "Man, what I wouldn't give for her bone structure!"

Ruth was waiting for Winifred in the bar of the Four Seasons. Winifred shuddered when she suggested a before dinner brandy. She looked at the waiter and said, "House white wine, please." She was echoing Aristelle's words, but she sounded knowledgeable and sophisticated.

"Christ!" Ruth exclaimed. "You look good enough to eat!"

Winifred felt her cheeks burn as she remembered being kissed over every inch of her body by the woman who was teasing her in what seemed to be an intentionally suggestive way. *Not on your life*, Winifred thought.

While they waited in the cocktail lounge for a table, Winifred sipped her wine. Ruth had two more brandies with no apparent effect. There was an awkward pause. One of them had to begin a conversation, so Winfred asked, "So, what are you doing now?"

"Making an effort to win back the love of my life," Ruth said.

Winifred was confused. "Didn't you say that you were waiting for a divorce?"

"I am referring to you and me."

"I didn't leave you, Ruth. You chose to leave me," Winifred said keeping her voice low.

"And it was the biggest mistake of my life! We were happy!"

A waiter appeared to guide them to a table. He put Winifred's wine and Ruth's brandy on a tray and ushered them to the dining area. Winifred opened her menu wishing the trend of this conversation not continue.

Ruth persisted. "So, weren't we happy?"

Winifred drew in a breath and then met Ruth's eyes. "I imagined I was happy; obviously, you were not."

"I was just claiming my independence—Oh, that's not true, at least not one hundred percent. We would have been social outcasts, and I wasn't mature enough to cope with that then."

"And I was? Back then I never considered anything other than the commitment I felt."

"And love?"

"I don't know how to define that now. I was barely out of my teens."

"But can you deny that there is something left for us to build a future?" Ruth was pleading.

The waiter appeared at the table. "More wine? Another cocktail?" Winifred declined but Ruth said "I'll have a refresher."

"Are you ready to order, or would you like a little more time?"

"I'll have the Tahitian shrimp and rice," Winifred said.

"The same," Ruth handed the waiter her menu. She hadn't looked at it.

They sat in awkward silence. Once the dinner was served, they picked at their entrees although Winifred thought the dish was uncommonly good, but Ruth's proposal had dampened her appetite.

"Winifred, can't we try again?" Ruth pleaded.

Winifred needed to find the words to tell Ruth that she felt compassion for her. She knew from bitter experience that the pain of rejection was excruciating. She herself had recovered emotionally;

her wounds had healed. Giving Ruth any hope would be dishonest, but she did not want to be harsh. She spoke gently and slowly. "I don't believe a fire that has turned to ashes can be rekindled."

"Isn't there an ember left?" Ruth asked.

"Too much time has passed. I'm a different person, and so are you. I had to fight to live though separation from you. Forgive the literary comparison, but I had to resurrect my very soul from the ashes like the Phoenix. I don't think I could go through that again. I wouldn't even want to try."

"So that's it, then?" Ruth didn't disguise what had turned from a pathetic plea to a tone of contempt. She grabbed her purse and stood abruptly. "You are heartless. I hope you'll live to regret it."

She nearly collided with the waiter who came with their bill on a tray. "My friend was late for an appointment," Winifred said lamely, and put two fifty dollar bills on the tray. It was enough for the meal, drinks, and a tip.

As she drove home Winifred replayed the conversation in her mind. Even the first year she was in England, she would have gone back to Ruth's embrace not walking but running. No more. She didn't feel anger, nor had she wanted revenge—that dish best served cold. She was, simply put, in another place. If there had been the fire of first love lying dormant in the cocoon that had protected her until she emerged from its confinement, she didn't believe she would have permitted it to blaze again.

Back home she removed her "spiffy" outfit, returned Aristelle's things and slipped into her well worn flannel pajamas. She welcomed the freedom to crawl into bed early without having to make an excuse. As comfortable as she was with Aristelle, there were advantages to solitude. "Good bye, Ruth," she whispered to the night.

Aristelle wouldn't be home for another week. Winifred had promised Helen that she would spend some time in Bellingham, but first she needed some physical activity to shake off the oppressive mood that lingered after her confrontation with Ruth. For two days she cleaned and polished. She straightened out kitchen cabinets and cleaned the refrigerator. In the latter she found some particularly nasty bowls of unidentifiable leftovers. Aristelle was not slovenly, nor was she, but neither spent much time "deep cleaning" as old Annie used to say.

When the floors were waxed and the refrigerator gleaming after having been scrubbed with hot water and baking soda, Winifred looked around with satisfaction. She had even cleaned the windows and removed an accumulation of ashes from the fireplace. *I could get a job as a scrub woman*, she thought.

Helen and Mildred were pleased to see her. Helen was smiling provocatively and Mildred, behind her, inclined her head to Helen until Winifred got the point. The braids which Helen had worn about her head like ropes were gone. She looked years younger with a stylish short cut softly framing her face. Her nose, elegantly Roman, appeared less severe with this new look, and she was smiling broadly.

"Wow!" Winifred exclaimed.

"My stars and garters," Helen said, quoting one of Grandmother's favorite phrases, "One would think that Dr. Eldridge would have come up with a more sophisticated remark that that!"

Winifred put her suitcase in her old room. In the evening, as she sat with Mildred and Helen playing Parcheesi, she was relaxed and content. The years had eroded all the rough edges of her adolescent anger.

They spent the next day with the horses. Winifred saddled her old mare which proved to have more life than either of the ancient geldings Helen and Mildred rode. When they came to an open field, Winifred asked if they would mind if she took a gallop.

"It's been a while, Winifred, don't fall off," Helen said.

She didn't. She cantered her mount some distance away from the others and then urged the mare forward. There was that peculiar smell of early autumn in the air when Indian summer was giving way to the promise of frost to come. It was a heady scent, far more intoxicating than wine or…she didn't want to think about it—brandy. After a few minutes she turned the mare back and rejoined Helen and Mildred at a gentle lope. "That felt so good!" she said.

The visit itself had felt good. She was home in so many ways: home in the center of herself; at home in the old family house; and at home in Seattle with the unpredictable, no, *irresistible* Aristelle.

Aristelle came home to the waxed and polished house. When she took her suitcase to the basement storeroom, she saw the rows of jars Winifred had canned. She was speechless, but found many words of gratitude when Winifred came home from the university.

In the evening there was a chill in the air, and Aristelle built a fire. "Good God, even the fireplace is clean! I am absolutely stunned."

They sat in front of the hearth, Aristelle in her recliner and Winifred on the couch with her legs tucked under her. Aristelle was reading the newspapers that Winifred had saved for her, and Winifred had a current novel. Warmed by the fire, they sat in comfortable silence. Suddenly Aristelle put down the paper. "Wasn't it Irene Bentley with whom you boarded in undergraduate school?"

"Yes. Why do you ask?"

"You might want to send her a condolence card."

Winifred felt a chill of foreboding. "What happened?"

"Her niece, Ruth, committed suicide day before yesterday—rather dramatically from the Aurora Bridge."

"Oh, my God," Winifred's breath caught in her throat. "I had dinner with her last week."

Winifred had lost all color. She got up, but swayed. Aristelle was certain she was going to faint. With a swift movement, she went to her and eased her back on the couch sitting beside her. "She was your friend?"

Winifred nodded. "She was my roommate before she went east to medical school at Cornell."

"I'm so sorry. Did she seem depressed?"

Winifred did not answer directly. "I may have killed her."

Putting her arm around Winifred but wise enough not to make a comment or ask a question, Aristelle waited. Winifred might need to say more, but she would not invade her privacy.

Finally Winifred spoke. "She was my friend and I would have given her the world had it been in my power. I stayed at the University when she left for Ithaca—how's that for symbolism? Aunt Helen and I hadn't resolved our problems and my father and his wife were in Montana. Ruth was friend, family and confidant."

"And much more I would assume," Aristelle said with infinite gentleness and not a trace of condemnation. "How old were you?"

"Nineteen. Ruth was five years older. When she left for New York I was heartbroken and incredibly lonely, but I counted the days until we would be together for vacations. But each time I planned to go back east, she would have a reason why it wouldn't be a good idea— family, her work, and other excuses. I flew to New York only once for a brief visit, but we hardly had any time to ourselves. So I waited until I passed my orals, and then I hoped we would finally have our summer in Europe."

"Did you?"

"No. The afternoon that I received the offer for my Fulbright grant, Irene Bentley told me that Ruth was coming back to Seattle to be married. I'll never forget that moment. Irene was gushing about how wonderful it all was and how I would surely be the maid of honor, and why on earth had I kept the news a secret? I remember stammering something as if I weren't surprised, and then I flashed my grant letter. She couldn't see the date. I lied about having to leave immediately."

Winifred continued to describe the shock, getting drunk in the hotel room, and deciding to go to Oxford. "The rest you know," she said.

"And she called you soon after I left?" Aristelle asked.

"A few days after. She wanted to go someplace "spiffy" as she called it, and we met at the Four Seasons. By the way, I borrowed your shawl."

"You were more than welcome to do so."

"Ruth had flunked out of medical school, divorced her husband and he was awarded full custody of their one child. The point of the dinner was to renew our relationship."

Aristelle waited.

"I turned her down. She had several drinks while she waited for me, and two more before dinner. She didn't show any signs that alcohol had affected her. I sipped white wine while she tried to persuade me that we could simply forget the nine years that had passed, and begin again. When she understood that I wasn't the Winifred she had known, she left abruptly—leaving me the bill. I didn't mind that. She turned back to me and said I was heartless, and that someday I'd look back and regret it. I guess I deserved that parting remark."

"You did not!" Aristelle exploded. "That was the last desperate ploy of a classic manipulator. I'll bet you she slowed down waiting for you to follow her and beg forgiveness. You were not responsible for her act of despair."

"I feel responsible."

"I understand. But the reality is that you proved to her that you were your own person, in charge of the life you made for yourself, and you proved to yourself that you possessed the wisdom not to retreat into a second adolescence. "Aristelle rose from the couch. "If you were anyone else, I'd offer a medicinal brandy, but I'm fresh out of Listerine, and knowing what you've told me, you'd refuse. However, I have a lovely old bottle of Drambui Liqueur, and I think a sip is in order."

By the time Aristelle returned with two glasses of the bronze liqueur, Winifred had composed herself. She knew her tears would come again, but for now the weight of guilt was lifted by her confiding in Aristelle. "I shouldn't have let myself inflict that whole story on you," she said.

"I'm glad you did. Sometimes the past, especially that which is tightly confined in memory needs to be let go. It seems to me that releasing the locked up experience may free you from guilt and regret—if not immediately, eventually. Your relationship with Ruth was both simple and complex. You needed someone to fill the void of your loneliness. You gave your love with loyalty, but you were young and vulnerable. Ruth was not, as you realized in her thoughtless disregard of you, the person you loved. She was an illusion."

"Thank you for understanding," Winifred said simply, sipping her liqueur.

"You're not alone in keeping secrets, my dear. As a doctor of literature you must recall Charlotte Bronte's lines, "The human heart has hidden treasures, in secret kept, in silence sealed."

"Yes. From "Evening Solace."

"I must confess to you that your coming to live with me brought back a flood of memories. I well remember sitting here the evening after we first met and reliving a period of my life when I first realized the theatre meant more to me than being a history major."

"You majored in history?"

"Two and a half years of it until I transferred from UCLA to the University of Washington and a drama program."

"That was quite a switch—geographically and subject wise."

Aristelle told her of her role in *The Doll's House* and her father's transfer at the beginning of World War II. "That was a good memory, but the eleven years after was not. That painful time of my life still troubles my dreams if not my consciousness."

Winifred waited to see if Aristelle would continue.

"It took years for me to come to terms with my own past. Bitterness still festers, and unlike you, it is not the aftermath of having loved or trusted. My father, a high ranking career army officer, had been transferred from San Francisco to Fort Lewis at the outbreak of the war. He insisted that I move north with him and mother. I gave in to his demands to my everlasting regret.

"It wasn't leaving UCLA that I regretted; I found that at the university here there were opportunities in my major and in drama. But my father created situations in which I was paired with his young adjutant, Judson Morgan. It was my first dating experience—at twenty-one. I had led a sheltered and controlled life. It took just one sexual encounter—not even one in the heat of infatuation and certainly not love, but, how shall I describe it?—one out of curiosity and long habit of submission. In those days no one thought of protection, and I hadn't considered the consequences. As you may guess, I found myself pregnant.

"Judson's concern was not for my reputation; he was terrified that his chances for advancement would be affected when my father knew of my condition. I couldn't even begin to imagine how angry father would be, nor did I want to contemplate the depth of my mother's disappointment in me.

"Judson had the solution. We would elope. He didn't love me; he didn't even respect me. He used my pregnancy to ingratiate himself with his colonel, and solve a family problem by saving my reputation. The problem was his mother, Abigail Morgan. She was widowed living alone in this house—the Morgan family home. If we married I would be her companion. Judson said that the house was within walking distance of campus, so I could continue my studies. This assurance was blatantly deceitful. He was well aware of the extent of Abigail's disability."

"Would you have married him if you had known?" Winifred asked when Aristelle had paused in her narrative.

"I could think of no realistic alternative. My own mother was thrilled, and my father was delighted that I had chosen marriage over a career. Judson saved his reputation, by purposely deceiving me. His mother's condition was not merely ill health, but a decreasing ability to care for herself with the complication of dementia. We would call it Alzheimer's today. For eight long years I was Abigail's nurse. I provided constant care for all her personal needs from bedpans and meals to basic hygiene: a twenty-four hour a day obligation. Gail was born seven and a half months after the marriage. She weighed a little less than six pounds, so we called her 'premature.' Judson wanted to name her after his mother—heaven knows why since he had shown no affection for her. We compromised with 'Gail' rather than 'Abigail.' "

Aristelle paused in her narrative to stoke the fire. Winifred took the opportunity to ask, "But didn't Judson at least help you when he was home?"

"No. The distance from the base was a long drive. We didn't have the freeway in the forties, only Highway 99 which was two lanes. When Judson did come home, which was seldom, I was there to satisfy his lust. Nothing more. I was trapped. Could I have left him and the stressful circumstances? I had no means of support; and I had Gail. God forgive me, I was happy when Abigail died in May of 1950. Gail was seven.

"That summer the Korean War was declared—the "police action," as we were led to believe. There were two major changes in my life. Both my father and Judson were dispatched to Korea; and my mother came to live with Gail and me.

"It was a godsend. With my mother to help me, I returned to the university and was able to complete my degree, a double major: history and drama. For the first time in years I was free to be myself. It was like breaking out of prison. By the time the peace agreement was signed I had begun my Master's Degree. The drama department offered me a position as an instructor, and I was accepted for a PhD program.

"The conflict in Korea finally resolved, and my father, now Lieutenant General Arnold, was assigned to Germany. He and mother left at the beginning of summer 1955. Then Judson came home. The first words out of his mouth were 'I want a divorce.' I was no longer useful to him; the fact that I had given all those years to caring for his mother as well as having given birth to his child, meant nothing.

"I wasn't surprised that he wanted to end the so-called marriage. He was not going to re-enlist, and he confessed that he was in love with a woman with whom he had had a relationship for years. They intended to live in Spokane where Judson would have a position in her father's business. He said he'd pay alimony for the sake of Gail, but I had another idea. I proposed instead to forego all claim to alimony or child support if I could remain in the house. I insisted upon a formal contract: Judson agreed that for as long as I would pay all taxes, maintain the house and property, and assume the remainder of the mortgage, the agreement could not be dissolved. Judson included a clause which stated that if for whatever reason I were unable to fulfill the terms of the contract, the house would revert to him without any compensation to me. I believe he thought that it would be sooner rather than later since he couldn't imagine I would be able to meet the terms of the contract. Who was I? —Just a woman, and one without any substantial income.

"Judson demanded joint custody of Gail. While he had never given me more attention than his physical needs required, he doted on her. Encouraged by Judson, his new wife beguiled the child to the extent that by the time she was in high school she badgered me constantly to let her live with her father in Spokane. Gail claimed I never loved her, only my work. I knew it was adolescent emotion speaking, but I finally gave in. From that time on Gail lived with her father and seldom visited me.

"I had my name legally changed from Morgan to my maiden name. I was determined to separate myself from the past. When I finished my doctorate, I accepted a professorship in the university's drama department. Sadly, my mother died in Germany, and I saw father only occasionally after he had retired to southern California.

"To this day I am haunted by my failure as a mother. Perhaps it motivates me to be concerned for my students. Anyway, my dear Winifred, now you know about the past that I have not confided to anyone else."

"Aristelle, I didn't expect you to confide in me because I had poured out my soul! But I am so grateful that you did. I see now why you're so careful about every little detail of repairs and yard work."

"Gail and Greg know of the contract, and they visit not to see me, but to discover anything that might justify having the house go back to Judson."

"But the thousands of dollars you must have invested in this house! Surely they realize the sacrifices you've made."

"They will tell you that I've had 'free rent' which is amusing to put it kindly. No, it is Gail's contention that an apartment would be more than adequate for a single woman, and that I am depriving her father of his family heritage. Ironically, if I had not spent almost eighty percent of my income on taxes and upkeep, I might have been able to buy another home. Yet I have to admit I love this place and the way I've furnished it over the years. If I had the savings to purchase it myself I would, in a heartbeat."

Winifred retired to her room feeling comforted by the shared confidences. Aristelle remained in her chair near the hearth until the flickering flames were faint embers. She placed the screen securely against the fireplace, put out the lights and walked slowly to her bedroom. *Yes, I shared part of my life, but not the treasured secret in my heart.* She touched the locket that she never removed from around her neck. Its solid gold had not tarnished, nor would the memory of Edna Lief ever fade. *In secret kept; in silence sealed...*

Aristelle was concerned that Winifred seemed uncharacteristically withdrawn. Perhaps "without enthusiasm" would be the better description. The shock of a friend's suicide would be reason enough for depression, but not for this long. They were well into the fall quarter. Aristelle believed she was still feeling a measure of guilt. It was not reasonable, but feelings are not always controlled by logic. Time would be the ultimate healer, but in the meantime Aristelle wished she could invent some kind of distraction that would help. Two weeks before the quarter's end, one presented itself by way of an extra project she had taken on. Aristelle had agreed to supervise a junior theatre major as he directed his first college level play. It was a simple minded but entertaining script by Agatha Christie, *Ten Little Indians*. It was not a profound social statement or *avant garde* piece, but a production that challenged a director and his crew in several ways—properties for one. An essential element in the conclusion of the play was a bear rug. The student director and his equally inexperienced property mistress could not find one. Aristelle recalled some photos Winifred had shown her of George and Marion's home on Flathead Lake. She was certain she remembered a bear rug.

While Winifred made a salad for dinner, Aristelle prepared a casserole. After she put the dish into the oven, she heaved a great sigh. It caught Winifred's attention as it was designed to do.

"What's that for?" Winifred asked.

"It's this damn student directed play. I have to hold Lewis' hand every step of the way. Metaphorically, of course. He's a handsome lad, but forty years my junior and I am not a cradle robber. Anyway..." She had Winifred's attention. "He's flummoxed by one challenge. He needs a bear rug for the final scene and no substitutions will do. He can't find one."

"My father has a bear rug—Grizzly, no less, in his den. Would you like me to call him to see if he'd lend it for the play?"

"Please!"

George was happy to be of help. Marion hated the rug and she suggested they donate it to the drama department for future use.

"Perhaps we could drive over there at Thanksgiving break to save the freight," Aristelle suggested thinking that the trip would be another distraction.

"Any other time of year, but with snow in the mountain passes and the fact that even under normal conditions it would be at least six days total coming and going, I think we should just have it shipped." The bear rug arrived by train, and Winifred was given the credit for a successful search.

"Since you're so good at tracking down impossible items, how about giving me some help with *On Borrowed Time?*" This was Aristelle's current production.

Winifred was familiar with the play which denied power to Death while he was trapped in an apple tree. "Please, Aristelle, don't tell me you need a tree?"

"In a word, yes."

"All right. That pathetic excuse for a cherry tree out by the garden shed hasn't produced a cherry since I've lived here. Why don't you chop it down?"

"But it's a cherry tree—the bark is different."

"So, have your crew sand it, smear some plaster on the trunk, paint and fake it."

"What about leaves?"

"I'll look for something plastic at the Salvation Army store or a floral supply," Winifred offered.

The former was a dead end, and the latter unreasonably expensive. Aristelle suggested that they ask the decorators in some of the major department stores if they had anything the university could borrow. Frederick and Nelson, a Seattle fixture, was pleased to lend them greenery in exchange for acknowledgement in the program and some publicity photos. In her spare time Winifred helped the property team staple the strips of leaves to the tree which a stage crew had placed in a sturdy frame which could hold the weight of the Death character. She was honored at the after production party which Aristelle hosted. The cast commissioned an art student to design a scroll with beautifully illuminated calligraphy: "Only God and Dr. Eldridge can make a tree!"

During the months of winter quarter Winifred recovered from the shock of Ruth's suicide. Aristelle believed her involvement with the plays had helped.

Winifred mustered the courage to visit Irene Bentley. During their conversation Winifred learned that Ruth had many problems. Even before she came to Seattle to enter a pre-med program, she had been treated for depression. She had faced the same problem in Ithaca. She was abusing alcohol as well. Irene confessed that it was she who had urged Ruth to contact Winifred. She believed that renewing the friendship the two once had would help her niece.

Winifred could not tell Irene the details of that last dinner meeting. "Ruth had hoped," Irene said, "that perhaps you might want to live with us again, but I did warn her that those carefree days of school couldn't be brought back."

Carefree days? Winifred thought. *Hardly. It was Let's Pretend gone sour.* They didn't meet again.

Winifred had been promoted to an associate professorship by 1973. There were four women in the English Department, but only one other in line for tenure and full professorship. Of these two only Winifred could be defined as a legitimate scholar. Her competition was Flora Fuller, a woman who knew how to take advantage of her physical attributes. She had shapely legs, strawberry blonde hair, and features some called beautiful. Winifred didn't agree. She looked at Flora's thin lips, eyes set too close to her nose, and her habitual way of tilting her head. The woman viewed everyone in a way that defined "looking down one's nose at the world."

Larry Hardin, a colleague, commented to Winifred that while the woman seemed professional and competent, she had the substance of a marshmallow. "Behind her back some of us call called her "Professor Fluffy Full-of-Herself."

"That's mean," Winifred told him.

"I suppose, but as her female competition, you'll learn what her sugary sweetness covers up. Personally, I'd rather be charmed by a cobra."

Winifred had no illusions about the disadvantages of being a woman in a man's world. Academia wasn't as exclusive as the Boy's Club of the Roman Catholic Church, but it came close. Winifred's dissertation, which was published by Oxford University Press, gave her an edge in spite of her youth; she was thirty-four, ten years Flora's junior. Publishing was vital in academic life and directly related to tenure and promotion. Flora Fuller had also published. Her book, *You Can Be a Poet Too*, could be found in high schools and Flora had the audacity to put her book on the required list for her Introduction to Poetry class. She rode high on its popularity, but her colleagues dismissed the work as shallow. When Winifred's publication of her dissertation was released, the department chairman left copies in the faculty reading room. Flora was unimpressed.

"Heavy reading" she said as she hefted the volume giving a cursive look at the dust jacket. "Had you heard that my book is in its third printing?"

"Congratulations, I don't think mine will make it that far," Winifred said pleasantly.

Across the room Professor Norgaard lowered the pages of the University of Washington *Daily*. "I hear it will be published in a German and Italian translation. Of course, its value will be appreciated only by authentic scholars." He retreated behind the paper. Flora had no come-back.

Winifred had missed two faculty meeting without having given an explanation. Notifications for these obligatory sessions were placed in the cubicles for inter office mail. She made no excuse, but she had received no reminder in her mail. Professor Larry Hardin caught Flora taking the latest notice from Winifred's box.

"Hey!" he said as Flora headed for the door. He said nothing more but as she looked back at him he folded his own announcement and slipped it in Winifred's box. Catching up to Flora, he said "Nice try, Fluffy. Better luck next time." Later in the day he recounted the incident to Miss Burke, the department office secretary.

"Dr. Effinger is too decent a gal to be submarined. Maybe you could put meeting notifications in a plain envelope? Or better yet give them to her personally."

Miss Burke peered over her wire rimmed spectacles. "Thank you for that word to the wise," she said pursing her lips.

Winifred was a natural born teacher. She could reach students at the top level as well as those who looked upon English literature or the Shakespeare requirement as a waste of time. Winifred convinced them otherwise. "Let these characters come to life," she'd say. "Consider this: they have flaws and foibles; some are fools; many are wise, and some are evil. Many are men and women we could honor today. The common denominator is that they are human. Shakespeare is more than a Sixteenth Century playwright; he speaks to us of the human condition."

By the end of the academic year, Flora had left to become the chairman of the English Department of a large public school district, and Winifred became a full professor with tenure. Aristelle was delighted as were Aunt Helen and Mildred. Over the phone Helen said, "I'm proud enough to burst my buttons!" Aristelle proposed a celebratory vacation at summer break. Neither she nor Winifred would be teaching during summer sessions. "Would you be interested in a week on Orcas Island in the San Juans?" She asked Winifred.

"I'd love that! When?"

"Gail is coming to stay with us while Greg goes fishing with clients in Alaska. He promised to take her to Hawaii when he returns. He'll be gone for ten days beginning this Friday. I'll arrange reservations for the day after they leave. That will give us the better part of August for a well deserved vacation."

Winifred disliked Gail, but she never gave Aristelle any indication of her feelings. Privately she characterized Gail as a combination of *King Lear's* Goneril and Regan. Winifred took some of Shakespeare's themes lightly in the spirit of "tongue in cheek." The theme that one might look through those windows of the soul and fall hopelessly in love was a tradition she thought was silly. Love at first sight was one of the characteristics of courtly love which she had described in her dissertation. When Winifred met Gail it was far from love at first sight; she looked into the eyes of instant hatred. She couldn't deny this awareness; it was visceral and unmistakable. Was it jealousy? How could that be? In no way did her living with Aristelle interfere with the fragile mother-daughter relationship. At any rate, she didn't want to be a part of the coming visit.

Winifred was setting the table for dinner when Gail arrived. She decided to use the Spode and Aristelle's sterling silver. She made an effort to be cheerful and hide her awareness of the antipathy Gail made no effort to conceal.

"I'm sorry I won't be home while you're here, Gail," she lied. She added that she was on her way north to spend time with her aunt.

"You have a family of your own?" Gail asked.

"Yes. My aunt lives in Bellingham. My father has a home on Flathead Lake in Montana."

At dinner while Aristelle cleared the table and went to the kitchen to make coffee, Gail remarked, "You seem to have a nice little housekeeping arrangement here with my mother."

"Yes. I appreciate it, believe me."

"Oh, I believe you."

Winifred did not like the tone of Gail's voice. Aristelle came from the kitchen with dessert. She wondered what part of Gail's pointed questions Aristelle had heard. Winifred stayed at the table long enough not to appear rude. "If you ladies will excuse me, I think I'll take advantage of this clear evening to drive north. Traffic can be bad in the morning."

As Winifred left the room she heard Gail ask, "Is she going to take your car and leave us without wheels?"

"Gail!" Aristelle reprimanded her. "Winifred has her own car. You didn't see it because she rents our neighbor's garage. Why would you think she'd take mine?"

Aristelle planned to entertain Gail with a variety of activities. They attended a play at the repertory theatre, visited the art museum in

Volunteer Park, and took in a British film at the University District's Varsity Theatre. Aristelle knew that her efforts to entertain Gail would not prevent her from bringing up the subject that was a recurring theme: the house.

"Keeping this place is ridiculous, Mother. It's far too big and the upkeep must cost a fortune. Why not let us sell it and you could get out from under taxes and maintenance?"

"That would certainly not be an advantage to me! It took me twenty years to pay off the mortgage—which was not easy. What I now pay each month is considerably less than rent in an apartment, and what would I do with all my furniture? Also, Gail, you know that I gave up the right to be compensated. Selling would not be wise economically, it would be foolish."

"Did it ever occur to you that Dad needs the money? You're taking unfair advantage of him by being stubborn."

Aristelle didn't respond with anger; she said calmly, "Who benefited for years by my assuming the mortgage, paying all the taxes, and keeping the house in good repair? I have a legal document which states that in exchange for all of that—which has amounted to more than the house will appraise for, I may remain here as long as I am able. Your father agreed to the settlement in order to avoid alimony. I will not have one cent in return in the event the house reverts to him, or to you as his heir. Why would you press me to give up my home?"

"There's more to it than that. You'd probably want to move if it wasn't for your boarder."

"Winifred and I manage very well, and the advantage is mine, not hers. You and Greg certainly understand that it is expensive to maintain a home."

"I understand that, but it is disgusting the way you two act like an old married couple!"

"What does that mean?" Aristelle knew very well what Gail implied, but she wanted her to give an answer.

"It's Edna Lief all over again."

With difficulty Aristelle remained aloof. "Yes. I recall your making the same comments when Edna was here. You know how ill she was; of course I wouldn't leave her alone."

"That's not the point. The two of you were chummy for years. I'm surprised you left yourself open to whispers and rumors. They must be flying now!"

"Let's get right to it. You and your husband think I am a homosexual?"

"If the shoe fits, mother." Gail said belligerently.

Aristelle looked at her daughter and then laughed. Nothing could have unnerved Gail more. Her reaction defined having the wind taken out of sails. "So with your impressive credentials in psychology, you have diagnosed my relationships with Edna and Dr. Eldridge?"

"I'm not totally ignorant of such things! Our church teaches us plenty about sin and sodomy."

Aristelle laughed again. "Daughter dear, I don't have the physical equipment to commit sodomy and I would rather not continue this conversation. You may play God and judge those who are less perfect in your sight, but stay the hell out of my personal life." With that, she went to her room closing the door behind her.

Early in the morning Aristelle awakened when the phone rang. When she came into the kitchen to make coffee, Gail told her that Greg had called to say he would return earlier than he had intended. "He's picking me up around noon, and we'll stay at an airport hotel tonight. He got us a flight to Hawaii for early tomorrow." Her tone was formal, and Aristelle responded in kind.

"That sounds like a practical plan. I should say good bye now as there are things I have to attend to at the university, unless you two would like to stay to dinner?"

"No, thank you," Gail said coldly.

At least she isn't in the habit of mushy farewells, Aristelle thought.

Gail's words disturbed Aristelle. Did they have an element of truth? Was she using Winifred as a substitute for her beloved Edna? No, she was not like Ruth, a woman of twenty-five seducing a lonely and impressionable girl of nineteen. If at any time Winifred decided to leave her for a career advancement or marriage, Aristelle would in no way interfere. She would endure the loss of her companionship. To stand in her way because of the affection she felt for her? Never.

Yet there was more to her disquietude. Gail had touched a nerve. She had cast her mother in a real life *Children's Hour*, and though the ages were different in Lillian Hellman's drama, there was more truth than speculation in the comparison. Aristelle could deny such feelings to Gail, but she was honest with herself. She loved Winifred, this exceptional person, with a depth that had taken her unawares.

Should she be honest with Winifred? Would confessing what she felt mean the end of the satisfying life they enjoyed? Truly, she didn't know. Perhaps the truth would break an emotional umbilical cord and free Winifred to explore a variety of possibilities for her future. *The truth will set her free*, she thought, but admitted to herself that if Winifred did leave it would plunge her into a deep well of loneliness. She had floundered in those dark waters before, and it had taken years to find the light.

The first year that Aristelle taught at the university, she had directed *The Sound of Music*. In spite of the detailed description in the director's script, she felt inadequate to coach her student actors in the folk dance sequence. Normally in a musical there would be a dance director, but aside from one other scene involving the character of Rolf and the oldest Trapp girl, this was not a "dance" show. The physical education department offered a folk dancing class, and Aristelle asked Edna Lief, the instructor, for help. Edna took over the dance sequences competently and enthusiastically. Edna loved the theatre, and she and Aristelle began to attend the symphony and theater together. Aristelle had an eye out for potential drama scholarship candidates, and Edna was good company when she went to productions at nearby colleges and high schools. Since Gail had left to live with her father, and Aristelle's home was large, the two decided that it was economically advantageous to share the house.

Aristelle had traveled overseas when Colonel Arnold was posted in Germany. She had been able to see France, Spain, and England. After her marriage to Judson, travel had been out of the question. She couldn't afford to leave while she had the burden of Abigail's care. When she was alone after Gail left to live with Judson, there was the mortgage to consider and the upkeep of the house. The summer after Edna came to live with her, she and Aristelle went to Europe with a university hostel program. Aristelle, at thirty-six was not in prime shape for a bicycle tour. Edna, far more athletic, encouraged her. Aristelle managed, but after their first day of riding, she complained to Edna, "I am certain that there are a hundred muscles in the human body I was never aware of."

During their years together there had been shy approaches to intimacy—holding hands at a movie or while driving to work, and even a brief kiss good night. Gradually this became love making. Aristelle had never been sexually satisfied with Judson. He was inconsiderate and rough, and when he became attracted to the woman for whom he left Aristelle, he ceased to require intimacy of her. She had not been disappointed. With Edna she gave love and affection and received the same from her. But this was short lived. Edna began to suffer from what she called "sick headaches." Soon her balance was affected. The doctors at Swedish Hospital diagnosed an inoperable brain tumor. She died within six months of the diagnosis. They had been together for ten years.

Edna had been raised in a succession of foster homes, and had worked to put herself through the university and graduate school. Since Aristelle was her only family; she took a leave of absence, and devoted herself to Edna's care until she died.

With Edna gone, Aristelle returned to her work. She was not a recluse, nor would her professional obligations allow her to withdraw, not to mention the fact that she needed the means to support herself. She maintained a professional relationship with her colleagues, some of whom she called friends, but she avoided the depth of friendship she had enjoyed with Edna. When she told Elizabeth Hopper that she was considering sharing her house, it was not that she desired companionship; she had realized that the expense of keeping an older house in prime condition was beyond her financial capability if she were to have any accumulation of savings for retirement. She had not intended nor had she anticipated that during the years of sharing a home with Winifred she would become emotionally involved. This was a truth best concealed.

Part Four

Winifred swept in the door with the sweetness, Aristelle thought, of fragrant summer roses. She had enjoyed the time in Bellingham, but enough was enough, she told Aristelle.

"They kept me so busy I hardly had time to…"

"To what?"

"I was about to make a vulgar remark."

"So make it! Don't leave me in suspenders!" Aristelle teased.

"Well, I hardly had time to pee."

"Now how on earth would you, a Shakespeare scholar, blush at such an innocuous expression? I know you haven't missed the point of the Bard's deliciously bawdy humor!"

"Point taken. When do we leave for Orcas and how can I help?"

Before Winifred arrived home, Aristelle had made lists, shopped, packed boxes of groceries and was eager to begin the adventure. "Wouldn't you rather wait a day or so before anther long drive?"

"No. Helen and Mildred told me about Orcas and I can hardly wait. I feel like a kid before Christmas."

They drove north in a drenching rainstorm. "How are your spirits now," Aristelle asked, "dampened?"

"Vision impaired," she said gripping the steering wheel, "but still enthusiastic."

The bad weather was an advantage. They had left at 4:00 a.m. to be in line at Anacortes for the international boat which stopped at Orcas on its way to Victoria, British Columbia. It was not uncommon for motorists to wait for hours before boarding a ferry when there was a crowd. They were lucky that on this stormy day the line was short.

By the time they arrived at Orcas Landing, the rain had stopped and the sun appeared in patches of blue as scudding clouds blew inland. By the time they reached East Sound, the weather was mild. They purchased perishables at the grocery store and then drove past Horseshoe Bay to the resort where Aristelle had reserved a "deluxe" cabin. Deluxe in cabin standards meant electricity, a full bath, stove, refrigerator, one bedroom, a hide-a-bed plus comfortable chairs and a dining table.

The resort owner, a bewhiskered gentleman met them at the main clubhouse. He was distressed. The cabin his guests had reserved had sustained major damage in a fire which also burned a cluster of smaller cabins. Apologetically he said, "I have only one place to offer you ladies—at half the price, of course. Or I could call Rosario, but that's three times as costly. I could also call Deer Harbor, but they don't have as nice a beach." He showed them a small but quaint cabin with an enormous fireplace, a little wood stove, a couch and a hide-a-bed.

"Is there indoor plumbing?" Aristelle asked apprehensively. He showed them the bathroom which was no larger than a closet. "You'll have running water, and out on the porch there's an ice chest."

Winifred's vacations with George and Marion had prepared her for the camping out style of cooking. She found a heavy iron frying pan that fit the wood stove top. It was perfect for two steaks. By the time they had eaten, it was almost dark and their host, whom they had dubbed Mr. Whiskers, was at the door.

"I forget to tell you. We turn off the generator at 11:00 o'clock. I brought you a kerosene lantern. It gives pretty good light. You can even read by it."

In spite of the pioneer accommodations, Winifred and Aristelle relaxed and, as Aristelle put it, played. They built bon fires on the beach, and even though it was August, they bundled in sweaters and blankets and fixed picnic meals.

"Hot dogs have never tasted so good," Aristelle remarked.

At low tide they browsed on the beach gathering shells and agates for which the rocky beach was famous. Winifred discovered a fossil in a split chunk of sedimentary stone. "Look at this!" It was an image of a beetle-like creature the size of her hand. "I'm holding a relic from a hundred million years ago."

"Possibly more," Aristelle said looking at the perfectly preserved form.

"It would give your creationist son-in-law the willies!" Winifred said.

One misty morning they drove to the top of Mount Constitution and from a tower on the grounds watched the fog lift revealing a panorama of islands below, the still waters crimson in the sunrise. On the way down the switchback road to sea level they counted fifty deer feeding in the early morning. The gift of a clear day was brief. By the time they reached their cabin a drenching rain had reduced visibility drastically. "So much for the reputation the islands have as the banana belt," Winifred said.

Cabin bound, they spent the remainder to the day reading and playing Parcheesi. If any time could be said to be a good time for truth and confession, the solitude and intimacy of their week together was that time. Winifred had insisted that Aristelle sleep in the bed near the wood stove. She used the couch in front of a window which was drafty and cold at night. One evening after they had sat up late while Aristelle read aloud, Winifred asked Aristelle if she would mind if she pushed the couch nearer to the hide-a-bed. "I'm shivering myself to sleep."

Aristelle was tempted to ask her to crawl in with her, but she didn't dare. How could she tell Winifred that she longed to hold her close; how could she find the words? It might be "truth" and "consequences," she thought, unsure of how Winifred would react. Aristelle chose silence.

Winifred wished she could let Aristelle know how close she felt to her. There were times, especially during this week, that she might have spoken, but she fled from the temptation of admitting a forbidden love. Paraphrasing Shakespeare, she feared to venture into Hamlet's country from where no traveler returns. She could lose her life not with the bare bodkin, but with rejection she could not bear. She remembered how Aristelle had praised her for not slipping back into adolescence when she had refused to renew the old ties with Ruth. Once during the past week, Winifred faltered. Aristelle had been reading one of the Bard's sonnets aloud. "When to the session of sweet silent thought I summon up remembrance of things past…But thy sweet love remember'd such wealth brings/ That then I scorn to change my state with kings."

Winifred's eyes had filled with tears which rolled down her cheeks. Aristelle said, "My dear—what is it?" but Winifred had brushed the tears away and murmured, "Nothing."

Aristelle said no more, but she believed Winifred had been thinking of Ruth. "Let's have a change of pace." And she opened a volume of *Leaves of Grass.*

Winifred finished her last student conference, gathered a stack of Blue Books, and hurried to leave her office for a quick lunch. She didn't see the figure in the hall through her clouded glass door before she rushed out. They collided and her exam booklets scattered.

"I'm sorry! Let me help."

Not until they had retrieved everything did Winifred get up from her knees to apologize for her haste. She looked at the man who stood tall beside her and cried, "Charles!"

"I had hoped to surprise you," he said grinning. "I didn't expect you to mow me down!"

"What are you doing on campus?" she asked.

"I'm a visiting professor for the summer. I'll be teaching a seminar on the politics of the New Deal. Do you remember Amy Mates from our side trips in the Cotswolds?"

"Of course!"

"She came to Michigan on a graduate project. One thing led to another and we were married last year."

"That's great. It will be good to see her again. Is she here with you?"

"No. She'll come when I find a house to rent. Right now she's in England. She misses her family."

Winifred looked up at him. She was accustomed to looking most of her male colleagues straight in the eye. Few were taller than she. "Aside from your distinguished graying at the temples, you've scarcely changed!"

"And you're as gorgeous as ever!"

Winifred blushed. "Is Hastings an Irish name? I hadn't known you were full of blarney."

"Sure'n begora, me mither was Dublin born, but me Da," he paused with a twinkle in his eye, "he was a glum Bostonian banker. So I've made use of both genetic attributes. Do you have time for lunch so we can catch up on the last ten years?"

"I don't have time today for more than a quick bite." I have a sandwich up in the faculty lounge and I have to look at these blue books before my 1:00 o'clock class. But are you free this evening?"

"Completely free."

Winifred gave directions to the house and then instead of going upstairs to eat, she went to the drama building in search of Aristelle. She found her in class. She hated to interrupt, but it was important to tell her she had invited a guest for dinner. Aristelle was delighted. "I'll stop at the market and get shrimp for my special recipe."

"That's a lot of trouble"

"Nonsense. You know how I love to cook."

The dinner conversation was entertaining and substantive. The three energized each other. Charles was sincerely interested in Aristelle's projects. A challenging production of John Osborne's *Look Back in Anger* prompted discussions about the British class system as compared to the United States. Winifred's planned book on

Shakespeare and the Principles of Power Politics inspired Charles to make a prolonged comment on Roosevelt's New Deal.

"We should sell tickets!" Charles said laughing. "Better still, let's get a major network to put us on T.V.—conversations round the dining room table."

After Charles had gone home Winifred put the dishes in the dishwasher while Aristelle took care of the leftovers. "We'll have to have him and his wife over when she comes out."

"That would be nice."

Amy and Charles were frequent visitors during the summer session. The night before they were to leave for Michigan Aristelle planned a special dinner. While Charles and Aristelle were involved in a spirited discussion of the Osborne play, Amy and Winifred cleared the table and prepared to serve dessert.

While they were alone in the kitchen, Amy said "You know Win, if you had given Charles half a chance back at Oxford, you'd be Mrs. Hastings, not I."

"Amy! I don't believe you!"

"You mean you didn't realize that he was—in American terms— smitten with you?"

"Heavens, no."

"You must have been as dense as the split pea soup Aristelle served us tonight." Amy said.

"But you two seem so happy—please don't tell me differently!"

"I won't. I plotted to come to Michigan. Then when we had gone out for a few months we discovered how much we had in common and what fun we had together. Finally the specter of Winifred Eldridge faded. Honestly, I was terrified when he was asked to teach here that he'd meet you again and remember old times."

"That hasn't happened, has it?"

"No. And I'm so grateful."

After farewells and been said and promises made to keep in touch, Winifred was glad to retire to the solitude of her room. Her conversation with Amy was not a subject she cared to discuss with Aristelle. She may have made protestation to Amy, but at Oxford she had noticed that Charles was making an effort to be more than just friends. Would she have responded to these indications if she had not been through the trauma of Ruth? It was a complicated question. She was fond of Charles, but in their many conversations it was clear that what would make him happy was a woman who would put her professional ambitions aside and give him a family. She remembered how relieved she had been when Charles returned to America, and she also recalled that Amy was not her usual bright self for some months.

Ruth may have initiated intimacy. Winifred herself would never have done so. Yet she had responded to her wholeheartedly. She couldn't avoid facing her orientation, but she would not share her realization with Aristelle. It was one thing for Aristelle to be sympathetic with her adolescent affair; but quite another for her to believe Winifred had not outgrown it. She thought of Charlotte Bronte's lines which Aristelle had quoted, "in silence sealed."

In 1980 Winifred celebrated her fortieth birthday. Aristelle had given her an "over the hill" party to which faculty from both the Drama and English Departments were invited. It was a merry affair in spite of the black balloons and equally funereal paper plates and crepe paper. The conversation turned to the cold war, the prospect of military build-up under a Reagan administration, and what most thought was a dismal state of the world.

"I've been thinking of doing Shaw's *Major Barbara*," Aristelle told the group.

"A little archaic, don't you think?" Larry Hardin of the English Department asked.

"Not if we consider the theme of the military/industrial complex," Aristelle said.

"Yeah, but Barbara caves in to the industrialist father," Larry countered.

Winifred said, "Shaw could have intended irony."

"Like Twain's 'War Prayer' or Swift's *Modest Proposal?*— Maybe. But it's tricky considering the political climate now." Larry said. "But, hey! If you do it, I'd like to play Barbara's father. It would give me an excuse to keep my beard!" Larry was thirty-two, but his youthful appearance made him look more like a student than a professor. He had grown the beard in the interest of presenting a mature, academic look.

"I just might ask you to do so," Aristelle said. "First I have to make sure I can find a Barbara from the current crop of actors."

Aristelle's hope to produce *Major Barbara* did not materialize. Instead, during the next year she directed *Mornings at Seven*, *A Majority of One*, and a series of one act plays. Aristelle began the school year unsure of a major production to precede her sixty second birthday. She came home one winter afternoon beaming. "I've found her, I've found her!" she exulted.

"Good God, who was lost?" Winifred asked.

"Barbara! In all the years I've taught I have rarely had such an experience. It was astonishing!"

"I thought you had given up on the play. You haven't mentioned it since my fortieth birthday party."

Aristelle put down her briefcase. "Do we have coffee? Let's have a cup and I'll tell you what happened."

They sat in the kitchen while Aristelle described an assignment for her second year drama class. "I've had *Major Barbara* in my head for years as you know, but I couldn't find a Barbara. Without betraying my intention, in every class I'd assign monlogues which would demonstrate quality I wanted. But what I got was never more than imitations of movie actresses. Then today we were listening to an assignment, and I found Barbara."

"The girl performed something from the play?"

"Actually, no. I sat in the back row expecting to hear another Portia speech or Juliet's death scene,—all the old standards drama students use *ad naseam*. This girl had edited a segment from *A Lion in Winter*. God forgive me, I thought was going to endure a Hepburn facsimile. But no! She gave the best interpretation I have ever heard from a student, and she obviously had the intelligence to edit the material. She shocked all of us, particularly me."

"So you think you'll do *Major Barbara?*"

"If Larry Hardin is still interested in playing the father; I don't have anyone else."

Aristelle held auditions and cast the play which was to be performed at the end of winter quarter. Before the blocking of action, Aristelle had a read through at her home. Winifred saw Aristelle's choice for Barbara, Stephanie Berman, for the first time. She was as stunned with the girl's appearance as Aristelle had been with her talent. The girl was slender, auburn haired with flawless fair skin and the cheek bones of a goddess. Winifred had to look twice at her large grey eyes to confirm that her lashes were hers and not false. To Stephanie's credit she neither flaunted her good looks nor attempted to be the center of attention. She didn't have to. She was. From the moment that this elegant creature walked into a room, all eyes were fixed upon her in admiration and wonder.

The subject of Stephanie and the play was a constant theme of conversation during the weeks of rehearsals. "Acting," Aristelle said, "is either an act, or a moment of transformation. With Stephanie we see only the latter. She could play Electra, Medea, or Cornelia in *Our Hearts Were Young and Gay* with equal believability! What a gift for a director!"

Aristelle invited Winifred to view the dress rehearsal, which she attended reluctantly. For the last two months it was all she could do to stop from saying, "Do we have to discuss Stephanie the Magnificent again, and again, and again?" But she held her tongue. Even Larry Hardin was bewitched. The afternoon of opening night he had stopped by Winifred's office. "You saw the dress rehearsal, isn't she awesome?"

"Stephanie?"

"Well, yes—certainly. I admit that she's a director's dream come true, but I meant Aristelle. I'd seen her productions, but I never appreciated her genius until I was one of her actors."

Winifred was happy to hear that Larry credited Aristelle with genius, but she wished he'd left it at that without adding to the litany of praise for Stephanie.

"Winifred," Larry said "why don't you try out for a production? It's fun to have faculty participation. One of these days you should convince Aristelle to do Shakespeare."

"How many reasons do you want me to give why I wouldn't dream of it? I'm a klutz; I have no voice; and I have the grace and flair of a turtle!"

"You underestimate yourself, Winifred. You inspire your classes, and let's face it, convincing an English Literature major that Shakespeare is as exciting as Dylan Thomas is an amazing achievement."

"Thanks, Larry." Any time Winifred thought of Stephanie she felt like a toad watching an angel take flight. She had to admit that she was jealous, wildly, passionately, screamingly jealous.

She gathered the bluebooks she needed to review during the weekend and left her office. Passing the faculty lounge a wave of memory washed over her. She remembered sitting across a long table facing the professors who were in charge of the oral examinations for her doctorate

Old Professor Wells had posed an interesting question. "Have you read Soren Kierkegaard, Miss Eldridge?"

"Certainly not in the original Danish, Professor, but I am acquainted with his work."

"Then relate what you read to your particular field, if you can." He had peered at her through spectacles perched at the end of his nose.

She collected her thoughts and then responded by comparing the philosopher's idea of a defining relationship with the mysterious person in Shakespeare's sonnets.

"Very well," the elderly scholar said. "However, I would like you to expand on the theme outside of Shakespeare." He lifted his eyebrows and waited for her answer.

As she considered her response, she remembered that one of her most stimulating experiences as an under graduate was this professor's Russian literature class. She took a deep breath, and launched into an analysis of *The Brothers Karamazov*. "Perhaps we may see an aspect of Kierkegaard's defining relationship in Aloysha and Father Zosima." As she continued to describe the layers of the philosopher's idea of relationships in other characters, the elderly professor steepled his fingers and smiled.

Why had she conjured that particular aspect of the examination now? It seemed like a non sequitur. Aristelle had left a message for her to stop by the drama building anytime after 4:00 o'clock. It was just a few minutes after three. Winifred decided to wait in the main library. The dimly lit gothic reading room fit her mood. It reminded her of Oxford and the years which had made such a difference in her life. She started to read a bluebook, but she focused inward, not on the page. If she looked into a mirror of truth, what would the reflection reveal? Would she see the image of a forty-two year old woman, successful professionally, but locked into a pattern of regression reminiscent of her infatuation with Ruth?

Her introspective mood was exacerbated by what seemed to be the beginning of the flu. She had felt vaguely nauseated all day. Perhaps it was a psychological effect; emotional conflict was commonly manifested in physical symptoms. She heard the rumble of thunder outside. Her painful probing into the dark corners of her soul was as depressing as the weather. Physical discomfort was getting in the way of clear thinking. Jealousy, infatuation, Shakespeare, Kierkegaard, and Dostoievski. Her disjointed thoughts were spinning out of control.

If she viewed herself as a character in literature about whom she was writing a critical analysis, what would she say? And why did her feelings for Aristelle have to be subjected to cold logic? The recollection of her oral examination might be her subconscious emerging to give her an answer. Relating her love of Aristelle to the ideal defining relationship made sense. The insight was like that light bulb hanging over the head of a cartoon character. In spite of feeling increasingly miserable, she had to laugh at the image. Looking at her watch she saw it was time to meet Aristelle. Fortunately, she had her umbrella, it was pouring rain and it was turning cold. As she walked to the drama building she remembered a line from Shakespeare: "Love is not love which alters when it alteration finds, or bends with the remover to remove." The rain had stopped, and the sun streamed through a break in the clouds. It seemed that nature was adding to the drama of the moment. In the sonnet there was the image of love as an ever fixed mark "that looks on tempests and is never shaken."

Yes, she thought. *It is not jealousy or infatuation that defines me, it is love.*

"I hate to ask you to do my errands," Aristelle said when Winifred came to her office, "but I don't have time to pick up anything for tonight's party. Would you mind stopping at the deli?—Nothing fancy, maybe shrimp, crackers or whatever, and then at least four bottles of champagne."

"You've never done that much celebrating after opening night—champagne?"

"This is a very special occasion." Whatever explanation Aristelle was about to give, she was interrupted by two girls from her costume crew. They had a problem with Major Barbara's uniform.

"You can depend on me," she told Aristelle, and started to leave. Before she reached the door Aristelle stopped her. "You looked flushed. Are you feeling all right?"

"I ate lunch over at the commons, and it's not agreeing with me. Don't worry, it's nothing a Tums won't fix!" She kept her voice light, but now she had cramps that weren't related to her time of the month.

She stopped at the liquor store for the champagne and then went to a delicatessen for plates of shrimp and several platters of veggies and dip. She knew there wasn't enough glassware in the cupboards for everyone so she bought little plastic champagne glasses which she found in the party section of the grocery store. At home she put everything in the refrigerator and then went upstairs to dress for the theatre. Under ordinary circumstances she would have gone to bed, but she couldn't disappoint Aristelle.

At the theatre Winifred sat in the back row by herself. She was feeling worse now than at any time during the day. She slipped out before curtain calls. At home she put the snacks on the dining room table, along with the little plastic champagne glasses. When Aristelle and the cast arrived, Winifred managed to congratulate them. Even through a cloud of pain, she was impressed with a marvelous performance. Aristelle drew her aside, felt her forehead, and sent her upstairs to bed. "I think you have a fever," she said.

"I guess. I have to admit I'm miserable."

"We'll miss you," Aristelle whispered, "but go on upstairs. I'll come up to check on you after everyone leaves."

Stephanie and Larry stayed to help straighten up when the cast and crew had gone. It was almost two in the morning. When they left, Aristelle went upstairs to find Winifred in a fetal position, moaning in pain. She hurried to the window at the end of the hall and called to Larry and Stephanie before they could drive away. Larry bounded up the stairs, took one look at Winifred and said, "We've got to get her to the hospital." Aristelle gave Stephanie the keys to her car, and Larry carried Winifred whom they had wrapped in a blanket to his station wagon. Aristelle sat in the back holding Winifred who was burning up with fever. The University Hospital was ten minutes away, and when they had parked outside the emergency entrance, Larry rushed in to alert the staff.

In the waiting room Larry and Stephanie stayed with Aristelle until the doctor on call came from the examining room.

"Dr. Eldridge is a very sick woman," he said. "Are you her family?"

"No," Aristelle said. "She has an aunt in Bellingham and her father is in Montana."

"We're prepping her for surgery. She was able to sign a consent form, but I'm not sure she knew what she was doing. We can't wait to find out. It could be her appendix, but we can't be sure. I've seen ruptured ovarian tumor exhibit these symptoms."

"Does she have cancer?" Aristelle asked dreading the implications.

"We'll find out when we do surgery. If it's the appendix, it may have burst; if it's the ovary we'll have the tissue and make a definite diagnosis."

"May I see her before she goes to surgery?" Aristelle asked.

"It might help her to know that someone is here for her—yes. But we'll be taking her upstairs shortly."

Aristelle approached the gurney where Winifred was hooked up to monitors and an I.V. drip. She took the hand that was free, and whispered her name. Winifred's eyes fluttered open.

"I'm right here," Aristelle said, "and the medical staff is going to take good care of you."

Winifred was in less pain, but the morphine prevented her from speaking clearly. She mumbled "I don't want to die before I…"

"You are not going to die, my love," Aristelle said firmly, but she felt the chilling fear that had overwhelmed her at Edna Lief's diagnosis so many years ago.

"But I have to…I need to tell you…" The sedative took effect and she closed her eyes.

Aristelle was reluctant to call Helen at 3:00 o'clock in the morning, but she knew she must. Mildred answered the phone and without hesitation told Aristelle they would leave for Seattle within the hour. Aristelle gave her directions to the university's hospital and said she would be waiting for them. It would take four hours at best for them to get past the early commuter traffic and the ongoing freeway construction between Bellingham and Seattle.

"We'll wait with you," Larry told Aristelle.

"No," she said, "I should lie down on the couch and try to take a bit of a nap. "I'll call you when I know more." She wanted to be alone.

When Helen with Mildred arrived, Winifred was still in surgery. The three of them sat in the waiting room, Helen clutching Mildred's hand, and looking ten years older than her sixty-nine years. Finally the doctor approached them. "Good news. It was the ovary, but there is no malignancy. We have her in intensive care for observation."

"May we see her?" Helen asked.

"Only family members are permitted in intensive care."

"All three of us are her family," Helen said.

The doctor smiled. He wouldn't challenge the lady especially with a patient as ill as Dr. Eldridge. "Go in one at a time, please, and don't stay more than a few minutes."

When Helen and Mildred returned to the waiting room, Aristelle gave them the key to her house, and told them to go on ahead. In the intensive care room, she went to Winifred's bed and stood aside while a nurse adjusted the drip and checked her temperature. "It's down from earlier," she said. "That's good news."

When she was alone with Winifred, Aristelle leaned closer to her. "It's Aristelle, dear."

Winifred pressed her hand weakly. "I'm glad you're here. I need to tell you..."

"There's nothing you need to tell me now. Just rest and concentrate on recovering."

"No—I needed to tell you—I'm so sorry. I've been jealous but I understand..."

"You understand? Oh, my sweet Winifred. Did you believe that she or anyone else could ever take your place?"

Winifred nodded, tears filling her eyes.

"Of course you had no way of knowing! Our celebration last evening was to announce that Stephanie and Larry are engaged. They'll be married!"

"Stephanie and Larry?"

"Yes! He tells me it was love at first sight—I know you don't believe in that, but in this case it is absolutely true! Of course ninety percent of the males in the drama department were equally besotted, but Larry had the edge!" Aristelle brushed Winifred's dark hair from her forehead, dark hair that had some strands of white. She bent to kiss her. "I love you, my dear. No one else comes close to your place in my heart."

Part Five

Aristelle and Winifred sat in comfortable recliners under the shade of a beach umbrella. They had set their reading aside to watch The Hardin children, eight year old David and four year old Monica, build a sand castle. Stephanie and Larry waved at them as David called, "Aunty Win! Aunt Ari! Come help us!"

"Go ahead," Aristelle said to Winifred. I'll stay here with my scripts."

Winifred joined Stephanie and the children. Larry's part of the project was to haul water from the low tide line. "I missed out," he said to Winifred as she joined the group. "Architecture is clearly my true calling."

"In your next life, perhaps, dear." Stephanie said. "Why don't you go keep Aristelle company for a while?"

Winifred and Aristelle were delighted to have become honorary aunties. "I had an Aunt Harriet when I was growing up," Larry told them. "She wasn't a blood relative, but a part of our family."

Stephanie commented that she would have loved such a relationship. "But my parents never stopped yelling at each other long enough to cultivate an extended family." She thought to herself that while her children called her friends "aunty," in her own heart their names would be prefaced by "angel."

Aristelle, now Professor Emeritus Arnold, retired only in the sense that she did not have the obligation of classes. She directed one or two plays a year for the Repertory Theatre or the university, and an occasional production for smaller groups. At present she was considering *The Madwoman of Chaillot*. She would have done the latter enthusiastically if Stephanie could have been the lead character, but the Hardin family was growing, and her former student's first priority was her husband and the children. This year Winifred had insisted that Aristelle do just one play in the coming autumn after having a siege of the flu and then pneumonia earlier in the year. Stephanie and Larry had urged them to spend two weeks with them during the summer in Cannon Beach, Oregon. "You'll have sunshine and the good salt air to give you strength for your next production," Stephanie told her.

"You young people don't need two old ladies crimping your style!" Aristelle answered.

"Hey!" Winifred said, "Speak for yourself!"

"As if a seven year old and a four year old don't already do the crimping!" Larry said. "If their Aunty Win and Aunt Ari were with us, we could leave them while we sneak off for whatever," he said winking provocatively at Stephanie.

"The 'whatever' is a euphemism for time to produce your third godchild," Stephanie whispered in Aristelle's ear.

The ten years after Larry and Stephanie were married had been bittersweet for Winifred. She and Aristelle had gained an extended family, but Winifred had lost hers. George and Marion died in the crash of a small plane over Yellowstone Park. Mildred passed away after a brief illness leaving Helen bereft and depressed. After several months of persuasion, Helen put the Bellingham house up for sale and agreed to live with Aristelle and Winifred. Winifred had hoped that it would help Helen to be with her only living relative, and also with Aristelle who was closer to her age. Unexpectedly, Helen's brightest moments were with the Hardin children. Helen had brought a trunk full of Winifred's childhood books which fascinated David. The first thing the boy would do when he entered Aristelle's house was to run to the library to search through the Little Golden Books and bring his favorites of the day to Helen. He would be content to sit beside her while she read to him. Helen passed away in her sleep in her eighty-fifth year.

After Helen's death Winifred said "I wonder if dying from a broken heart is a concept with more truth than metaphor."

"I think it may be true, dear, but Helen lived a long life, and was ultimately happy," Aristelle said. "But let me say this: if when I leave you, you were to shrivel up like a dried piece of fruit, you had better watch your rear, for I will rise up from whatever after life I am in to kick you where it will hurt most!"

Frequently when Winifred came home from the university she would hear the children playing and smell the aroma of a roast and baked bread which Stephanie had prepared. The closeness with Stephanie and Larry made it possible for Winifred to accept invitations to conduct workshops and attend symposiums away from home. Aristelle was nearly an octogenarian, and although she was in good health, Winifred was reluctant to leave her alone.

One evening when the two families were together, the door bell rang. David, now a self sufficient eight year old, cried, "I'll get it" as he ran to the door. On the porch were two people he didn't know. Larry was behind him. The man and woman were well dressed, but rather somber. Larry's first thought was that they were Jehovah's Witnesses, but they didn't seem to have books and pamphlets with them. "How may I help you?" He asked.

"By telling me where my mother is!" Gail snapped.

"You must be Aristelle's daughter," he said. "Come in, please."

As they entered the house Aristelle came from the kitchen. "Gail and Greg! This is a surprise. Come in and take off your coats. We're just about to sit down for dessert. Stephanie made an apple pie."

In the kitchen Winifred told Stephanie, "It's Goneril or Regan— take your pick, along with Iago. I hope to heaven they haven't brought King Lear."

Stephanie smiled. She knew the play and she knew the story of Aristelle's ex-husband and daughter. She was also aware of Gail's constant efforts to convince Aristelle to sell the Seattle house. Gail was so persistent in this request, that when George and Marion's

Flathead Lake property came to Winifred, she thought of suggesting to Aristelle that they move there. Two considerations prevented her from acting on the impulse. First, Aristelle loved her theatre work and secondly, the medical facilities were not the quality of the University medical center.

"I think we should gather the kids and disappear," Stephanie said.

"No, please! They may be reasonably civil in front of you."

"This is a surprise," Gail said as she and Greg sat down for dessert. "She fixed her gaze on Larry who was putting Monica in the high chair he had moved from a corner of the dining room. "Do all of you live here?"

Larry replied pleasantly. "We're what you might call adopted. Your mother and Dr. Eldridge are Godparents to Monica and David."

"How nice," Gail said flatly.

"Are you in Seattle on business or for pleasure?" Stephanie asked filling in an awkward silence.

Gail felt a gentle kick from Greg who sat beside her. She took it as a warning. They had agreed to broach the subject of the house carefully. "Actually, Mother," she said choosing not to answer Stephanie directly, "Greg has business in Portland, and since he had to come west of the mountains, I thought it might be nice for me to spend a few days with you, that is if you have the room."

"We don't live here," Larry said laughing.

"Nevertheless, they are family," Aristelle said.

"As it happens, there will be more room than usual," Winifred said. "I'm flying out tomorrow—to New York. I won't be home for a week, so you and Aristelle will have the house to yourselves."

"Dr. Eldridge is chairing a conference at Columbia University," Larry added. He didn't like the contemptuous looks this couple gave Winifred. "I'm also attending."

"I'm hoping that Winifred will keep an eye on him," Stephanie said trying to keep the tone light. "There's a growing number of young female PhD's these days!"

"Did you bring your suitcase in, Gail?" Aristelle asked.

"Greg and I will stay at the hotel tonight. He can drop me here tomorrow."

They left and Larry and Stephanie gathered the children. Winifred followed them to the porch and asked Stephanie to look in on Aristelle during the next few days. She and the children had been planning to stay with Aristelle, but obviously that plan wouldn't work.

Gail was uncharacteristically pleasant when the next morning she arrived to stay with Aristelle. Greg had strongly cautioned her that, in his trite phrase, you can catch more flies with honey than with vinegar. Gail was plotting her strategies. She was determined to use the time to convince her mother that she and Greg would be in serious difficulties if the money from the Seattle house were not available to provide the care Judson needed. His second wife's inheritance had been divided among four other siblings, and had not lasted. The house Judson lived in with his second wife was not theirs. They rented from her father. He had no claim of community property when she died. Now Gail would claim Judson desperately needed to be in a retirement facility.

For her part, Aristelle was determined to avoid controversy. Winifred had urged her to let the house revert to Judson. "There are any number of properties near the university district which would be suitable." However, they had agreed that moving would be a major task, and had postponed a decision. Winifred knew that they were facing an imminent problem. Aristelle was not in good health. Before she left for her conference she took the time to speak to Arthur Fleming Jr. Although he had retired and his grandson now headed the firm, he still advised long time clients.

"When I return, I want to make an offer for our house. I have a feeling Aristelle's daughter is determined to persuade Aristelle to let it go. That would involve legal documents, so please don't let Aristelle agree to anything."

Aristelle had planned to attend the theatre Monday evening with Stephanie, but Stephanie insisted that her ticket should go to Gail instead. In a rare climate of civility, mother and daughter spent a pleasant evening. They stopped for a late snack on the way home, and it was close to midnight when Aristelle parked the car in her driveway. As she climbed the steps, her attention was on locating her house key. Suddenly she missed her footing and fell backward down eight steps to the cement landing. The keys flew out of her hand and she lay still. Gail screamed which awakened the neighbor who came outside in a night robe. His first thought as he saw Aristelle's still figure was that she was dead. Aristelle had lost consciousness when her head hit the pavement.

Gail retrieved the keys and stood helplessly at the bottom of the stairs. "For God's sake, get a blanket," the neighbor shouted. "I'll call 911," Aristelle's right leg was under her body as was her right arm. The ambulance arrived within fifteen minutes, and by the time the medics had placed Aristelle on the stretcher, she had regained consciousness, but was in pain. Gail followed the ambulance to the university hospital.

Gail waited in emergency until the doctor had completed his examination. "Your mother has a compound fracture of her leg, a broken wrist, and a broken hip. She'll be in surgery for the leg and perhaps for the hip depending on her vital signs."

"Do I need to sign anything?" Gail asked.

"No. Professor Arnold was awake and able to sign the consent forms. She is on the university medical plan, but we would like a copy of her insurance card if you could bring that later this morning. When did your mother last eat?"

"We stopped for a strawberry waffle after the theatre—about 11:30 last night."

"All right. We'll give her a spinal."

"Well, I will leave her in good hands." Gail said.

The doctor thought that it was unusual that a daughter would not ask to see her mother, but didn't comment. She hadn't even suggested that the hospital call her when surgery was completed. Gail was eager to get back to the house. This accident was the answer to all the problems she and Greg had. It was obvious that Aristelle would not be able to care for herself or the house, and she would see to it that she found a nursing facility where her mother could go when she left the hospital.

At the house, Gail searched through Aristelle's desk and found Arthur Fleming's name and a folder with legal information. Gail had brought all the documents she needed for Aristelle to consent to turning the house over to Judson. With her father's power of attorney, she would see Arthur Fleming at his law offices as soon as she could get an appointment.

It was 9:00 o'clock Tuesday morning when she arrived at the hospital. Aristelle's room was in the orthopedic wing, and she was still drowsy after five hours in surgery. Her leg was on a sling, her arm in a cast, and pillows prevented her from turning. The nurse told Gail that a pin had been put in Aristelle's hip, and that it would be at least a week before she would be able to sit in a wheel chair. She left without seeing her mother; her first priority was her appointment with Fleming.

The attorney was sorry to hear of his client's accident. After she made a good showing of concern, Gail came to the point of her visit. "According to the terms of mother's contract with my father, the house reverts to him in the event that she can no longer keep it up or live there."

"Has she considered a 24 hour nurse?"

"She's just a few hours out of surgery and groggy with drugs. I'll wait until later this afternoon to talk to her. Home care would be excessively expensive and might be necessary for months. I'm going to arrange for a convalescent home."

"That, too, would be very costly, but I must inform you that temporary incapacitation in no way breaks the contract your mother has with Judson Morgan. And you must have your mother's authorization before you move her to a nursing facility."

This seemed to deflate Gail. She had been so certain that she and Greg could take advantage of the accident.

Fleming continued. "For you to make arrangements without Professor Arnold's consent, you would have to prove that as a result of the accident—the physical shock to a woman of her age, her judgment was compromised. Of course you may be able to convince your mother that it is in her best interests to do as you advise." Remembering his conversation with Winifred before she went to New York, he said, "In the event that your mother would agree that maintaining the house and property is now beyond her strength, I do know of an interested buyer."

"Who is it? Give me a name; I would like to contact him immediately!"

"The prospective buyer is out of state." This wasn't a lie—just a slight misrepresentation of fact. "First, you must have your mother's consent. I would suggest, if I may, that you wait until this afternoon when she will be alert and make your proposal to her then." He wanted to speak to Aristelle before Gail could get to her. Gail's eagerness to sell might work to Winifred's advantage. He decided to say more. "Do you know what a 'quit-claim' is?" he asked.

"No."

"Basically it is a risk to a buyer and one which I would not ordinarily suggest, but in the case of your father's house I am certain that everything has been well maintained, and there are no liens on the property. It means your father must sign a document giving the deed to the buyer who would assume all the risks. He would avoid an agent's fee and the expenses usually assumed by the seller. The buyer would pay him the full amount of the agreed asking price in a bank draft which is the same as cash. In our present economic downturn, if the house were put on the open market, an interested party might have difficulty obtaining a mortgage. My client will not have to apply for a loan. Now I'm not promising anything, but if you wish, I will pursue the matter—with the understanding that your mother must agree,

"That would be ideal! I will talk to her."

"Wouldn't it be more thoughtful to wait a few days?"

"Our father's situation is urgent, Mr. Fleming, but I will wait until this afternoon."

"What about your mother's furniture? Did all of that come with the house, or has she bought pieces of her own? And does her boarder have any claim on furnishings?"

"We will have mother's furniture stored. As for the boarder's. She'll have to figure that out for herself."

"Do you have a copy of your mother's rental agreement with this person?"

"I didn't see anything in the papers I brought to you, so evicting her shouldn't be a problem."

"Verbal contracts are legally binding. The fact that you found nothing in writing does not mean this person has no rights. But it is pointless to speculate until we know if your mother will consent to leave her home."

After Gail had left the office, Arthur Fleming pondered the situation. Aristelle's house would be an excellent investment for Winifred with a measure of poetic justice thrown in. He would contact Winifred, who probably did not know of the accident, and then go to the hospital to speak to Aristelle.

Gail left the law offices eager to contact Greg and tell him that there was a possible buyer if Aristelle would consent to sell. She called him as soon as she entered the house. "Well, talk to your mother immediately," he said, "while she's facing a long recuperation. Play on her independence. Convince her how humiliating it would be to have to depend on that Winifred gal. She'd be unlikely to take over as a nurse. Tell her you'll find a rehabilitation facility."

"I'm going to see her this afternoon. You'd better get back here."
"I'll get a flight from Portland first thing tomorrow. It's your job to convince your mother."

Winifred and Larry had left for New York on a noon flight Monday morning. Stephanie thought it would be best to let a day or two go by before dropping in to check on Aristelle. She was certain that Gail would not appreciate her visit, certainly not with the children. Monica had pre-school Tuesday and Thursday, and David was in school. It was a good opportunity to stop by.

Aristelle was a "morning person," frequently up and having coffee by six thirty or seven. By the time David was on the school bus and Stephanie had dropped Monica at the Montessori school, it would be nine, late enough not to disturb Gail if she were a late sleeper. When no one answered the doorbell, Stephanie was concerned. Aristelle's car was in the driveway, so they were probably at home. Before she could decide what to do next, Gail had opened the door, She was in a robe, bare footed, and there was no tell-tale smell of coffee—Aristelle's get up and go fuel for the day, as she called it.

The first words out of Gail's mouth were, "It's nine in the morning for heaven's sake!"

Stephanie replied with good humor, "I'm sorry. Aristelle is always up early. Does she have a rehearsal?"

"Well, not today."

Stephanie was immediately concerned. "Is she ill?"

"No. Just in bed." Gail commended herself on the misleading statement. Aristelle was most definitely in bed, she just didn't say where, and it was no business of this woman where she was or how late she slept. "I'll tell my mother you came by. —Stella, is it?"

"Stephanie," she corrected keeping a cheerful tone. "I'm sorry to have gotten you up—I'll come back later."

"We'll be out. We have plans. And we'll be gone all evening," she added. "Have a nice day!" and with this abrupt and insincere remark, Gail closed the door.

As Stephanie went down the steps, she was certain that this strange encounter meant something was very wrong, and she was seriously concerned. She drove to the campus and parked in Larry's space behind Padelford Hall. His student reader sat at his desk with a pile of blue books in front of her. "Hi, Mrs. Hardin!"

"Hi, Angela. It looks as if you're busy, but I need to ask you for a favor."

"Sure."

"I'd like you to dial Professor Arnold's number and ask to speak to her. If she answers just give the phone to me, but if anyone else picks up the phone, or if they ask who you are, just answer truthfully, but say you need advice since your boss is out of town."

"I'll put the call on speaker," Angela said as she got the number from Larry's rolodex. She wondered about the cloak and dagger approach. The phone rang for seven times before Gail's impatient answer.

"Yes, what is it?"

"May I speak to Professor Arnold, please?"

"Who is this?"

"This is Angela Petersen, Professor Hardin's reader. I, uh, need her advice on a paper I'm correcting since my boss is out of town."

Stephanie held up her thumb letting Angela know she was doing well.

"She can't come to the phone. Give me your message."

"Well, it's kind of complicated unless you know something about John Donne's Holy Sonnets?"

"No, I don't."

"When may I call back?—I really need to speak to Professor Arnold."

"I'd prefer you didn't. We'll be in and out."

"When will..." The phone clicked. Angela switched off the speaker and hung up the receiver. "Strange conversation," she said.

Something was definitely wrong. Stephanie decided to play detective. The street where Aristelle lived was divided and large maple trees were in the median. She parked on the opposite side from Aristelle's driveway where she could watch the house without being seen. Aristelle's car was still there. She waited for an hour before Gail came down the steps and got into the car. She was alone. Rather than waste time using her key to check inside the house, Stephanie decided to follow Gail. To her alarm, she drove past the emergency entrance at University Hospital and turned into the parking lot for visitors. When she had disappeared through the door, Stephanie went into the lobby and found a pay phone. She called Monica's school and told one of the teachers that she was unavoidably detained, but she would pick Monica up as soon as she could. Then she hurried back to her car to wait for Gail to appear which she did in twenty minutes. When Aristelle's car was out of sight, Stephanie went inside to the reception desk.

"I'm here to see Professor Aristelle Arnold, please?"

The receptionist checked her computer screen and said, "She's on the orthopedic floor."

At the nurse's station Stephanie stopped to ask which room, but was told that her daughter had requested that only Professor Arnold's immediate family be allowed to visit.

"Professor Arnold is my Aunt Ari," she said. "I know she'll want to see me."

The nurse followed her to Aristelle's room. "Professor Arnold, your niece is here."

"Stephanie!" Aristelle's voice was hoarse, but she was alert and aware of her surroundings.

The nurse left them. Stephanie pulled a chair near the bed. "I told her you are my aunt! Evidently Gail instructed that only immediate family visit. —Aristelle, whatever happened?"

Aristelle told her.

"Are you in much pain?"

"Some, but I'd prefer pain to the foggy stupor I was in after surgery."

Stephanie told her about the morning's encounter with Gail and how she had followed her. "I'll call Winifred."

"Arthur Fleming, our lawyer, has contacted her already. He came to see me yesterday after Gail spoke to him. We have a little drama going on. Arthur told me that Gail believed the house would be returned to Judson now that I wouldn't be on my feet. He described Gail's plan to send me to a nursing home so she could claim the house on behalf of Judson. You would have been proud of my acting ability. Knowing that Winifred was going to make an offer to buy the house for us, I said I was too weak and in too much pain to deal with any thought of returning home, especially considering the cost of care. I told her to do whatever she thought was best."

"She believed you?"

"In the vernacular, she fell for it hook, line, and sinker. Winifred gave her presentation yesterday and is probably flying home as we speak." Then she began to tell Stephanie the plan.

Gail had been delighted when Arthur Fleming told her that he had contacted the prospective buyer, and that the person was eager for the transfer of deed to be accomplished without delay.

"I'm worried about the woman who lives with Aristelle. Can she make trouble?"

"When I spoke to your mother just a few minutes ago," Fleming told her, "she assured me that there was only a casual agreement between herself and Dr. Eldridge about sharing the house. She was certain there would be no challenge."

"Winifred won't sue us or attempt to delay the sale?"

"No. I took the liberty of speaking to her as well. As a matter of fact, she has decided to purchase a home of her own."

"That's a relief. I really thought we were going to have trouble with that lady."

"You have convinced Aristelle that for the foreseeable future she cannot take care of herself. I'm sure you understand how difficult it will be for a woman as independent as your mother. I have made the arrangements necessary for her care as soon as she leaves the hospital. She does not want to burden you and your husband with the responsibility."

"I can't tell you how relieved Greg and I are—for the sake of my father, and my mother, of course."

Fleming rose to his feet. He was sick of this woman's not so subtle efforts to take advantage of her mother. "I will act in Professor Arnold's behalf and see to it that she has no worries that will impede her full recovery. You may trust me to make sure no one takes advantage of her." He did not add, "as you have done." He sensed that the woman was either too obtuse or self absorbed to understand that this was what he meant.

Stephanie met Winifred at SeaTac's luggage carousels. "We don't need to give Aristelle acting lessons, but her performance must have been academy award caliber!" Stephanie said. The second act in the drama would be to approach Gail at the house.

Gail was at the window watching as Stephanie opened the trunk of her car and removed Winifred's suitcases. Then, to her relief, Stephanie drove off. Gail met Winifred at the door. "She might have helped you with your luggage," she said.

"She needed to be home for her children. I'm grateful that she was willing to meet me at the airport. The taxi would have been expensive."

"So. I guess you've heard that we have a buyer for this house."

"Yes. It's too bad Aristelle won't be able to keep it, but all good things must come to an end. I'll make arrangements for my possessions so everything will be taken care of by Saturday." Winifred paused on her way upstairs and looked back at Gail. "How did you make the sale so quickly? I would have imagined it would take months."

"That's really none of your business." She challenged Winifred. "You haven't even asked me how my mother is. I find that heartless."

"Why? She's your mother, not mine." Winifred was enjoying this scene. Gail was dumbfounded. "If you'll excuse me," Winifred said, "I need to organize my things. Aristelle's lawyer told me that your buyer wants to have the locks changed before the end of the week. Can a buyer make demands like that?"

"He can do anything he wants now that everything is agreed. We'll need your key and any spares. Mr. Fleming insisted that I give him the ones I collected from my mother.

"I'm sorry, Gail, I need mine for the movers. Mr. Fleming told me to turn them in to him personally. He said not to worry about Aristelle's things. He has made all the arrangements necessary as your mother directed. May I ask where you plan to stay for the remainder of the week?"

"Not that it should concern you, but the buyer has arranged for Greg and me to stay at the downtown Marriot, at his expense."

"Amazing!" Winifred said, hoping she sounded sufficiently surprised. "Then I suppose I won't see you again. You'll be going back to Spokane?"

"Greg will be here to pick me up sometime later this morning. For some peculiar reason the buyer wants us to come back here to the house on Monday so he can hand over the check personally. For a quarter of a million we'd meet him in Timbuktu. Greg wants to thank him for putting us up at a first class hotel. We didn't expect that."

"I'm sure you're pleased by the fact that everyone is trying to accommodate you."

"Not that it's your business, but yes."

Winifred had to find a qualified nurse to help care for Aristelle when she was released from the hospital. This would be a challenge since there was so little time. Winifred was tactful when she interviewed nurses, and cleverly steered the conversation to matters of personal beliefs. One of the candidates attempted to impress her with her faith based motivations. "The Lord told me that this was just the job for me," she said. "In these cases of long recoveries it can help the patient to know that she is in His hands." This in itself wouldn't cause Stephanie to reject the woman, but she had added, "I read the Bible to my patients every day." Aristelle would not appreciate efforts to convert her.

There was another concern. There were those who would condemn the commitment Winifred and Aristelle had with each other, and it would be difficult for them to conceal their relationship from someone who would be in the house 24 hours a day, seven days a week for an indeterminate time.

She found a recently widowed woman who was highly recommended by Aristelle's doctor. She had done practical nursing before her children left home, and then had gone back to school for her R.N. She was knowledgeable, and she had had experience in physical therapy. Linda Countryman, was in her late forties and the ideal choice. She didn't appear to be a judgmental person, and she seemed genuinely concerned for the welfare of her prospective patient. At the end of their conversation it was Linda's turn to ask a question.

"You require twenty-four hour care for Professor Arnold possibly for months after she comes home."

Stephanie was quick to assure her that she and friends would relieve her as long as they knew what to do and how to give Aristelle the help she needed.

"That is not my concern specifically. Would she object to my having a visitor?"

"I wouldn't think so."

"I have to be honest with you. My son will want to see me. He is a wonderful young man, and a loving son. And he is gay. I love him and I have come to love his partner as well. Their situation would be quite evident to a person as astute as Mrs. Arnold. Would she disapprove?"

"I assure you, she would not. As you know, there are many men and women in the drama department who are openly gay, and not one of them has ever felt the slightest rejection from Aristelle Arnold. I would suggest that when you meet her, you should be as open with her as you have been with me."

Aristelle would be released from the hospital the Sunday before Gail and Greg would appear for their money. As far as Gail knew, her mother would go directly from the hospital to a nursing home. She said her good bye to Aristelle Saturday afternoon without even asking Aristelle where she would be. "You call me, mother, when you're settled."

"Yes, I will do that."

When Gail and her husband left the house to turn the keys over to Arthur Fleming, Winifred took the precaution of having the locked replaced lest Gail and Greg might attempt to reenter the house. Winifred drew all the curtains. Mrs. Countryman had brought some personal belongings but would not move in until Aristelle was brought from the hospital the day of the quit claim.

Act Three, as the conspirators called the final stage of the plan, began when Gail and Greg arrived, at the house on Monday. Fleming was already seated at the dining room table waiting for them. Winifred was out of sight with Aristelle and Mrs. Countryman in Aristelle's room. Aristelle was ready in a wheel chair for what she called her grand entrance. Gail seemed puzzled by the fact that the house seemed untouched; the furniture was still in place, and what was more disturbing. Winifred's car was parked in the driveway. "I thought the house was to be emptied? Tell me why the boarder's car here," she demanded.

Fleming ignored the question. "Do you have the deed signed and notarized?"

While Gail muttered under her breath, Greg handed him the document. When he was certain all was in order, Fleming handed Gail the bank draft for $250,000.00. Before she could read the signature on the note, Winifred entered the room.

"May I present the new owner," Fleming said. "Dr. Eldridge, I believe you have met Aristelle's daughter and son-in-law."

"What the hell?" Greg exclaimed. Gail stood gaping.

On cue, Mrs. Countryman wheeled Aristelle into the room. As a further surprise, Stephanie, Larry and the children appeared from their hiding place in the library and surrounded her.

"Isn't it wonderful how all this has worked out?" Aristelle smiled benevolently relishing the astonished expression on the faces of her daughter and son-in-law.

It took four months before Aristelle regained her balance and strength. She maintained a program of exercise faithfully even after her nurse had left the house. "Pretty good for an old lady!" She would say. When she began to walk with confidence with the aid of a cane, she participated in a trio of one act plays in which she took responsibility for one, leaving the other two to different directors. The work was healing in itself.

Winifred heard the commotion in the faculty lounge before she opened the door. When she entered the room, the silence was immediate. Larry, Professor Norgaard and Dean Bricker stared at her.

"Am I interrupting?" She asked.

The three were obviously uncomfortable. Finally Larry spoke. "Have you seen the *Daily*?

"No, I haven't. Who is protesting what?"

Norgaard handed her the paper, front page up. In broad headlines Winifred saw "Students for Moral Standards Protest Gay and Lesbian Faculty." Along with the article that followed was a three column print of Aristelle at an honorary banquet being hugged and kissed by Winifred. The caption read: "Lesbian couple flaunt their involvement."

"What on earth?" She looked at the others.

"Read on," Dean Bricker said.

The article claimed that a number of faith based student organizations proclaimed that known homosexuals should not display their deviant life style in public since their actions contradict the laws of the Judeo/Christian tradition and offend some students.

"This is idiocy!" Larry blustered." At least fifty men and women came up to Aristelle to give her a hug and a kiss at that event. —You among them, Dean. Shouldn't that headline have read, 'Dean of the English Department flaunts an extra-marital affair?' This trash doesn't warrant a comment by Professor Eldridge."

"I still maintain that Dr. Eldridge must write a letter to the editor with a strong statement of denial," Dean Bricker said. This was the opinion that had started the shouting match Winifred heard before she opened the door to the room. Larry had argued that it was inappropriate. "The university should not get involved in debating fanatics."

In answer to Dean Bricker Winifred said, "I can't do that."

"Of course you can't," Larry affirmed. "You shouldn't respond to these morons, it isn't their right to question you. For God's sake this is the twenty-first century, not 1600."

"I know that. Aside from this group's narrow mindedness, if I make a denial it would be pointless. And it would be a lie. You know that better than anyone, Larry."

Norgaard frowned. "You're admitting to being a lesbian?"

"Here is my non-denial denial: it is not any one's business. I am three years from retirement. Winifred looked at the Dean and said, "Dr. Bricker, do you believe this accusation is grounds for censure and dismissal of a tenured professor as this group demands?"

There was silence in the room. Winifred went to a work table and placed her pile of blue books on it. The three men stood in awkward silence not knowing how to respond.

"Well, no," he sputtered. He respected Winifred as a teacher and a scholar.

Winifred continued: "I wasn't aware that we had a 'don't ask, don't tell' policy at the university—in our department or in any other. Hypothetically," she continued, "suppose I am what this article implies, and suppose this has been true for all the years I have been a faculty member. How would that fact have affected my teaching, my scholarship, and my behavior toward my students and the faculty?"

"You are exemplary, of course," Professor Norgaard said.

Winifred turned to Larry. "Do you agree?"

"Good God, yes! This whole conversation is ridiculous. The place for this paper is in the garbage." He crumpled the sheet and stuffed it in the green institutional container.

"Then let's leave it at that, shall we?" Winifred said as she returned to her stack of blue books. Her eyes looked at the students' writing, but she wasn't reading. *So*, she thought, *the cat clawed its way out of the bag. Fine. Pour some cream in a saucer and let it soak its whiskers. I don't give the contents of its litter box what these righteous holier-than-every-one-else may think.*

When she arrived home, Winifred found Aristelle in the kitchen cooking supper.

"Aristelle!" Winifred cried, "You're trying to do too much!"

"Not at all. The *Daily* came in this afternoon's mail, and I'm celebrating the opening of the closet door! Do you mind terribly, precious?"

She went to Aristelle and put her arms around her. "No, I don't mind. But please, don't use that term of endearment—it makes me feel like a Tolkein character!"

There was very little publicity after the *Daily's* story. When the name of the home church for the anti-gay movement appeared in a follow-up, Aristelle commented that it was linked to Gail's church. "It would seem there is a connection."

"I hope not. What could be their grievance?" Winifred said. "She had her way and walked off with a quarter of a million dollars in her pocketbook. One would hope that would soften her attitude."

"Gail's protective armor is as impervious as any found on the planet. For her heart to melt, compassion would have to penetrate, and the likelihood for that is slim. Gail has been angry since she was very young, especially at me, and I'll admit to a measure of responsibility. In retrospect, perhaps I gave up on her too soon."

In the year that followed, Winifred saw that Aristelle was failing. It seemed as if her beloved was fading like a once brilliant photo turned from Technicolor to a sepia shadow of the original. They continued their customary evening reading aloud, but frequently Aristelle's book would slip from her grasp as she would fall asleep. As Winifred watched Aristelle deteriorate in all ways except her keen mind, she knew that their time together would be measured not in years, but in months. All too soon Aristelle's voice and loving touch would be a memory.

After fighting an influenza infection which turned into pneumonia, Aristelle died peacefully in her own home with Winifred by her side.

Winifred's grief seemed beyond her ability to cope. Some years ago Aristelle had told her how she had fallen into a deep well of loneliness when Edna Lief died. Now that she was gone, Winifred felt herself sinking in dark waters far below any light. She remembered that Aristelle had threatened to rise from the grave and give her a swift kick where it would hurt most if she ever wore a shroud of grief. "I can't help it, my dearest," she sobbed. "I just can't help it."

Stephanie and Larry refused to let her slip away from them. "We know what you feel though we realize that we'd have to multiply our grief ten fold even to begin to understand yours," Stephanie told her.

The memorial was in the new drama department theatre which had been named in honor of Aristelle, The Arnold Theatre. The space, though large, was filled to capacity and the fire officials had to look the other way when the aisles and the lobby filled. Her colleagues and friends expected Winifred to speak, but she had refused until Stephanie spoke to her.

"Aunt Win, you have to speak. There is no one in the world who should take your place. All of us who loved Aristelle need to hear a tribute from the one who knew her best. And loved her best," she added.

Winifred walked to the podium that had been placed in front of closed curtains. She prayed to whatever great power of the universe existed, that she would be granted the strength to speak.

Looking at the amazing number of people who had come to pay tribute to Aristelle, she began. "Aristelle would not be honored by our tears, and yet few among us can hold them back. They spring from our profound love and from our loss of a precious gift, a woman like the rare pearl of inestimable price. Aristelle would not have accepted that metaphor. Shakespeare said, 'But thy sweet love remember'd such wealth brings that then I scorn to change my state with kings.' We possess the riches of her talent, compassion, friendship, and love in our hearts. This legacy cannot be celebrated by tears. It is true that we will not hear that melodious voice, or see the smile that was a reflection of her genuine understanding of the human comedy. But the essence of the woman who is, yes, is Aristelle Arnold remains with us."

Tears filled Winifred's eyes, but her voice was strong. "I announce to you a tangible memorial: the Aristelle Arnold House, her home. It will not be preserved as a mausoleum, a mere reminder of a great woman. It will be filled with the voices of deserving students who will be given room and board there and tuition, as well. Long after Aristelle Arnold has become a name and not a personal memory, her spirit will continue in the young men and women who aspire to careers in the theatre's varied forms. These will include playwrights and actors; directors and producers; teachers, musicians and crafts persons—all who give us theatre. It is my hope that this legacy will be perpetuated through the gratitude of those who will have benefited from it. May Aristelle never rest in peace, but continue to inspire us."

There was a moment of silence as Winifred stepped down from the stage. Then, as of one mind, those gathered rose to give a deafening applause.

Alone in her home, Winifred took a small box that Arthur Fleming had given her after the memorial service. "I have no idea what this is," he said, "but I give it to you to fulfill Aristelle's wishes."

Inside, attached to a gold chain, were two gold rings intertwined and welded seamlessly together. It was the chain Aristelle had always worn. Winifred slipped it over her head. It hung close to her heart. A note was in the box:

> No power on earth can deny the union of two souls.
> We were not allowed to vow 'til death do us part,'
> But that did not affect the reality of us. Believe that
> Death is not as strong as love. —Aristelle.

Winifred thought of the rhyme that had impressed her so many years ago, but she changed the words: "Is she in heaven? Oh yes, I've heard tell; my dearest beloved, my Aristelle."